Contents

Index of Characters vii

Chapter 1   First Contact..1
Chapter 2   Damon and Ashlie................................13
Chapter 3   Return of Silver....................................26
Chapter 4   Separate 37
Chapter 5   Escape 48
Chapter 6   Dungeons 60
Chapter 7   Mysterious Fog 73
Chapter 8   Guinea Pigs 78
Chapter 9   Rescue 82
Chapter 10 Slowly Rebuilding 96
Chapter 11 Poisonous Waters 108
Chapter 12 Searching for a Cure 126
Chapter 13 Steel Weapons.................................... 133
Chapter 14 The Creature 147
Chapter 15 Preparing to Fight.............................. 158
Chapter 16 Fight or Flight 173
Chapter 17 Are They Safe?................................... 181
Chapter 18 The Island 195

An Unfinished Event

An Unfinished Event

New Territories

Jimmy Kerrison

PARTRIDGE

Copyright © 2020 by Jimmy Kerrison.

ISBN: Softcover   978-1-5437-5851-1
             eBook   978-1-5437-5852-8

All rights reserved. No part of this book may be used or reproduced by any means, graphic, electronic, or mechanical, including photocopying, recording, taping or by any information storage retrieval system without the written permission of the author except in the case of brief quotations embodied in critical articles and reviews.

Because of the dynamic nature of the Internet, any web addresses or links contained in this book may have changed since publication and may no longer be valid. The views expressed in this work are solely those of the author and do not necessarily reflect the views of the publisher, and the publisher hereby disclaims any responsibility for them.

Print information available on the last page.

To order additional copies of this book, contact
Toll Free +65 3165 7531 (Singapore)
Toll Free +60 3 3099 4412 (Malaysia)
orders.singapore@partridgepublishing.com

www.partridgepublishing.com/singapore

Index of Characters

Jenavieve Moon-Strong
Angalie Loupe Hole
Josh Cold
Jimmy Jamerson
Bellomie
Rosalie
Julien
King
Silver
Sam
Raven

Ashlie and Sarabella Moon-Strong
Leo and Isabella Loupe Hole
Lilly Cold
Damon Lufsberry
Theo
Billie
Roan
Ollie
Coralie
Bob

Chapter 1

First Contact

*O*verwhelmed, they all sat, crestfallen.

Looking out of the windows, they could see massive meteors hurtling towards the ground. Due to the turbulence, the plane kept hitting air pockets, making everyone sick. As the plane came closer to home, they saw massive craters in the ground; virtually everything had been destroyed. Only a few buildings remained intact.

"What the hell happened?"

"Everything's gone."

Two months ago, eleven lucky young people won a two-month trip to the wilderness to learn how to survive in extreme environments. They learned how to make and use weapons, how to light a fire to keep warm in the cold, and how to survive in some of the harshest conditions imaginable. Fitness training was a key element of the course. The conditions were very severe, but they learned a lot. The two months flew by, and the eleven were now flying home.

They sat in silence as the plane circled the airport and slowly descended.

"I think I can see someone," Jenavieve cried out.

A man was waving at the plane from the tarmac. The plane touched down and came to an abrupt stop, and the passengers all fell forward out of their seats. Smoke started to rise up outside the plane.

Pointing out of the window at the smoke, Angalie screamed, "Guys, look outside."

"I think the engine's on fire," Jimmy yelled, lifting himself up so he could get a better look.

"We have to get out," Julien said, as he, Josh, Bellomie, and Sam ran to the door and tried to open it. "We'll suffocate if the smoke gets inside."

Pulling and pushing at the door handle, Sam shouted angrily, "It's jammed."

"Guys, we've got a problem," Raven shrieked as smoke started seeping into the plane.

They could all see the smoke entering the cabin.

"What are we going to do?" Angalie asked, scared.

Silver scanned the windows and saw that the seal on one of the windows had cracked. "Lift me up. I'll try to kick open this window, but keep trying to open the door."

Jimmy and Julien picked her up, and she started kicking at the window.

Silver said, "Nothing's happening; it's stuck."

She continued to kick the window and shouted in frustration when the glass wouldn't give. She sat down and started massaging her foot, which she had injured trying to kick out the window.

"What are we going to do now?" Raven asked as the cabin slowly filled with smoke.

"Cover your faces and stay low," King ordered.

They all covered their faces with their shirts and knelt down as the plane completely filled with smoke.

Meanwhile, outside, the man had extinguished the fire in the engine. Inside the plane, some of the passengers thought they were going to pass out when all of a sudden, they heard a crash; the man had smashed open one of the windows with the fire extinguisher, and the smoke was escaping from the plane. As the smoke disappeared, they slowly got up from the floor. Looking out of the window, they now recognised the man outside: It was Billie, standing there with a big smile on his face.

"Sorry I couldn't get here sooner," he yelled. "I couldn't find the fire extinguisher."

"Let's go," Jimmy said. "Out through the window."

The window Billie had broken was large enough for them to escape through. Jimmy went first, cutting his hand on it.

"Ah, mother—! Be careful, everybody," he called back. "The glass is jagged."

They all got out of the plane and started coughing the smoke out of their lungs.

Billie spoke first. "I'm glad to see you're all okay."

"Where is everyone?" Angalie asked.

He replied, "They all ran when the meteors hit. Whilst you were gone, there were several catastrophes. Meteor showers left countless craters in the ground. Earthquakes shook the ground and cracked open the ocean floor, which released a deadly virus called Anoroc. The wind carried it inland from the sea, and once it was airborne, it spread fast; it killed its victims like the plague. It deteriorated the brain until there was nothing left. The people who inhaled it died immediately, but for those who drank it, death was slow and painful. Most of the people were killed by the virus, but some have been mutated. Those who weren't mutated, like me, had to find ways to survive."

"Oh, that's horrible. What terrible news," Jenavieve said, thinking about her family. "Why did you stay?"

"Someone had to get you back," Billie replied, smiling again.

"Thanks," she responded. "I need to find my sister and mother, so I can't stay here. Sorry."

"I understand. You should all try to find your families." Billie handed each of them a map from his bag.

"I guess this is where we all part ways," Jimmy said, shaking hands with everyone who was on the plane. "It was nice knowing you all."

Bellomie patted Jimmy on the back. "You too." He nodded and left with his sister Rosalie and Julien.

"May we meet again," Silver said. She turned and left, followed by Sam and Raven.

Billie was next to leave.

Before walking away, King said, "It was nice meeting you."

Jimmy looked at Josh, Jenavieve, and Angalie. He smiled and then announced, "And then there were four; ha ha."

"Ha ha, yeah." Josh smirked as they walked away.

It began to snow.

They all went their separate ways to see what had become of their families.

"Long walk home," Jimmy stated, hating the thought of the long hike through the forest.

"Let's go," Jenavieve replied. "We don't know these woods and what could be in them."

She looked at the map Billie had given her, figured out how to get home to Ville de Parie, and led the way, followed by Josh, Angalie, and Jimmy. The snow fell harder and began settling on the ground, which made it difficult for them to walk. They were dragging their feet through the snow when Jenavieve suddenly came to a halt.

Jimmy had fallen behind. "What is it?" he shouted.

Josh and Angalie caught up with Jenavieve and looked into the distance.

"It looks like a cave, which should protect us from the snow," Jenavieve shouted back as Jimmy caught up. "We can rest there for the night."

As soon as they reached the cave Jimmy suggested, "I'll try to make a fire. We can huddle together to keep warm."

"Yeah, good idea. I'll help you build it," Josh replied, kneeling next to Jimmy.

Collecting some twigs and leaves, Josh and Jimmy arranged them just inside the cave's opening. They tried to make a spark by clicking two stones together to make a fire. It didn't work because the stones were wet.

After a few minutes, Jenavieve grinned and said, "I have a lighter in my bag."

"You couldn't have told us that earlier?" Josh snapped.

"I wanted you to earn it," she replied, handing him the lighter.

"Earn it?" Josh muttered under his breath, rolling his eyes.

He clicked the lighter three times and lit the pile of dead leaves. They slowly caught alight. The four of them sat around the fire, Josh holding Jenavieve and Jimmy holding Angalie. It was dead silent outside the cave, and their fatigue caught up with them. They lay down and soon nodded off to sleep.

Outside, the moon was the only light. It got colder throughout the night. There were all sorts of noises, howling and screeching, coming from the dark. There were sounds of bats and nocturnal birds flying around just outside the cave. The fire burned steadily while they slept. It kept them warm; it also kept the creatures away. As the sun came up, the four of them woke at the same time. It had stopped snowing, but the ground was still covered in snow.

"Good, we're all up," Jenavieve said. "I checked my bag; there's some bread in it, but there isn't much. We will have to ration if we are going to survive on it until we get home."

The others all nodded. They finished eating and headed out for Ville de Parie.

As they walked through the drifts, Josh commented, "Wow, it snowed a lot last night."

"Yeah, and there were some strange noises too. Things I have never heard before," Angalie added, walking past Jenavieve to the front of the group, where some of the snow had turned to ice.

"Oh, you heard them too?" Jimmy said, catching up with her. "I thought you were sleeping."

"Yeah, well, we've never been in these woods before, so who knows what is lurking here at night?" Jenavieve spoke loudly so they could all hear.

Josh looked nervously to the left and then right. "Yeah, let's just try and get home before we have to encounter anything that Billie told us about."

"Why, you scared?" Angalie teased.

They carried on, dragging their feet through the heavy snow.

"Yeah, I am. You should be too." Josh kicked a big stone covered in snow to the side.

"Oh, hell no." Jimmy exclaimed.

They stopped and looked up at the mountain blocking their way.

"Yup. We're gonna have to go over it," Jenavieve said.

Angie stood still and stared at the mountain. "It's huge. It's gonna take us forever"

"C'mon, let's go," Josh said, taking long strides past the others.

It was warming up, and the snow had started to melt. It seeped in through their shoes and made their feet wet. Halfway up the mountain, Angalie was still moaning.

"Stop complaining," Josh said as he leaned on a tree to catch his breath. "We are nearly at the top, and then it's downhill, which will be easier."

When they got to the top of the mountain, the sun was shining brightly, and there was a clear blue sky. The four of them stopped and looked down the mountain.

"What is that?" Josh asked, pointing.

In the distance, they could see a hut, which looked like it had been damaged by the meteor strike. Standing next to it was a man.

Angalie asked, "Is someone there? Maybe he can guide us to Ville de Parie."

The man turned towards them but didn't see them. Jenavieve looked at him and said, "That's not a man anymore. Remember what Billie said?"

"Do you think it's a mutant?" Josh asked.

"I think so," Jimmy said. "We have to pass him to go on, but we have no weapons."

Looking down the mountain, Angalie asked, "What if he sees us?"

"I don't know," Jenavieve said as she started to walk down the slope, "but there are four of us and one of him. I think we can take him."

"Wait, let me check my bag," Jimmy called out. "There might be something we can use."

"Is there anything?" Angalie asked.

Jimmy zipped up his bag and slammed it down. Frustrated, he replied, "Nothing."

"Let's go down," said Josh. "I think you're right Jenavieve, we can take him; maybe he won't notice us."

The four of them took deep breaths and continued down the mountain. They each picked up a large stone, ready to fight the mutated man if they had to. As they neared the bottom of the mountain, clouds shielded the sun, but there was still enough light. The mutant had its back turned to them as they approached it. They looked at each other anxiously, thinking about what to do if it turned to face them. The mutant was eating what looked like a human arm. It was taking big bites out of it, like an animal.

"Let's try and sneak around him," Josh whispered, pointing with the rock in his hand.

"What if he hears us?" Jenavieve replied quietly.

The mutant sensed their presence. It turned quickly, dropped the human arm, let out an ear-piercing screech, and charged at them.

"Run," Jimmy yelled.

They took one look at the creature and ran.

Chapter 2

Damon and Ashlie

Back home in Ville de Parie, Jenavieve's sister Ashlie and her friend Damon were dazed as they stared at the scene. They were horrified by the damage that had occurred. They had to get away to somewhere safe. The two friends locked arms and began to walk with the hundreds of other people who were also seeking safety. The smoke from the meteors was drifting away slowly. Now there were dark clouds in the sky hiding the sun and it had begun to rain. Moments later it started pouring and the temperature dropped significantly.

"Stay close to me," Damon said. "We need to find shelter, or we'll get soaked."

The people around them started running in every direction trying to find somewhere safe.

"Look, we can get a little shelter there!" Ashlie said, pointing at the trees.

They jogged over to the trees and saw that a couple of people had the same thought; they were already in the sheltered spot. Ashlie and Damon walked on looking for a place to stay the night. The two of them were walking quickly and had left the others behind.

"There!" Ashlie said, indicating a sheltered spot.

"Nice, good eyes. We can spend the night there until it stops raining," Damon said as he scurried over. Ashlie was still close to him with her arm interlocked with his. It was late and had become dark.

They could see stars in the sky, Damon suggested, "We should get some sleep and head out in the morning."

Lying on the ground against her bag, Ashlie replied, "Okay."

"I'll try to make a fire to keep us warm but no promises. Although, I did get pretty good at it practising in the mines where I work." Damon said as he started gathering wood and leaves for the fire.

Moments later there was a small fire burning. Damon sat by the fire keeping warm. Ashlie lay with her head on her bag next to him and eventually fell asleep. Damon sat wide awake watching over her.

During the night, there were so many sounds. Damon just sat in silence ignoring them. In the morning, Damon could see the sun shining. He hadn't slept at all. He gently shook Ashlie's shoulder to wake her.

Sitting up, Ashlie asked, "Did you sleep?"

"No, I couldn't," Damon replied, getting to his feet and helping Ashlie up.

Walking outside the shelter with the sun shining on them, Damon asked, "You ready?"

"Yeah." Ashlie replied, looking up at the sky. The rain from the night before had stopped.

Ashlie asked, "Any idea which direction to go?"

"Yeah, I think it's this way," Damon replied, pointing in front of him.

There were puddles of rain everywhere and it was freezing cold. It started to snow gently. All the people from the night before were gone. The countryside was completely deserted for as far as they could see.

Looking around, Ashlie asked, "Where is everyone?"

Damon answered, "No idea. C'mon, this way," he said.

They entered a field. There were trees to the left and hills to the right. In front, the land was beginning to be masked by snow. They carried on walking through the snow. After hours of walking, they stopped when they came to a hill.

"Look, a house," Ashlie said, pointing towards the hill. The house had been damaged by the meteors, but it would provide shelter. "Do you think anyone is living in it?" she asked, heading towards the house.

"I don't know, let's check it out," Damon replied, walking behind her.

Ashlie continued, "It's damaged but will provide some shelter, I guess."

She entered the house and shouted, "It's empty!"

Damon followed her in and replied, "Take a look around, see if there is anything useful that we can use."

Ashlie walked into the back room and shouted," There's a bed in here!"

"Okay, I found some food!" Damon yelled from the kitchen. "The tap is still working."

"Why would anyone leave this place I wonder?" Ashlie asked, making her way to the kitchen.

"No idea, maybe they ran from the meteors." Damon mused, looking at her.

Looking around the kitchen, then walking into the front room Ashlie replied, "Yeah. Maybe."

Half of the front room had been destroyed by a small meteor.

"What should we do now?" Ashlie asked, turning back to look at Damon in the kitchen.

"I don't know. We can eat and rest here for now," Damon replied, looking at the food.

Walking to the kitchen table, Ashlie said, "Also I saw some clean clothes in the bedroom and a bag we could use."

Damon handed Ashlie a plate with some food on it. He got some for himself and joined her at the table and said, "After we've finished eating, we should get some rest."

"There's only one bed," Ashlie replied with a mouthful of food.

"We'll have to share. I'm not sleeping on the floor," Damon told her after taking a sip of water.

They finished their food and Ashlie replied, "Okay, I guess."

Damon suggested, "It's getting late. Let's get some sleep and then we'll head out in the morning."

"Yeah, good idea," Ashlie replied, walking into the bedroom and sizing up the bed.

"Which side do you want?" Damon asked. There were two pillows at the top of the bed and one blanket folded at the bottom. On the left of the bed was an open space where the window used to be before the house had been damaged by the meteor.

"I'll take the left," Ashlie replied, sitting down on the bed and kicking off her shoes.

"Okay," Damon said.

They pulled the blanket up and tried to get to sleep. Damon was exhausted and fell straight asleep.

During the night, there were lots of different noises coming from outside. Loud screechings came from the darkness. Damon slept through it. Ashlie lay awake. Her teeth chattered because of the cold. She was also frightened by the noises and was gripping the blanket tightly.

"Damon, are you awake?" Ashlie asked quietly, gripping the blanket tighter and pulling it up to her neck.

"Damon," she whispered again, a little louder, but he was fast asleep. Another loud screech came from behind the house followed by many more which woke Damon. He quickly sat up.

"What the hell is that?"

"I don't know," Ashlie replied fearfully.

Ashlie got out of the bed and walked over to where the window used to be. It was too dark to see anything. Damon got up and quickly pulled her shoulder down so that whatever was outside couldn't see her. The loud screeches roared again. Damon and Ashlie swiftly stepped back.

"I don't think it was the meteors that scared the people away from this house," Damon said in a whisper.

"Yeah, I think you're right," Ashlie replied, still shaking nervously.

"C'mon, we have to get out of here," Damon said, picking up his bag.

They were both very frightened. They ran out the front door. Damon took one look back at the house and saw what was making the noise.

"Let's go, fast, this way," Damon shouted, pushing Ashlie in front of him.

The creatures hadn't seen them until Ashlie tripped on a rock. They heard her fall, turned their way, let out a loud battle cry, and chased after them.

Damon helped Ashlie up and said, "C'mon, we have to go. How's your leg? Can you run?"

"Yeah, it's okay," she replied, getting up. "I can run."

They kept running as fast as they could on the uneven ground, with the creatures still in pursuit. In front of them was an open field, which led up to a mountain. Damon and Ashlie were breathing heavily, panting after every step they took. They could see their breath in the cool air. The creatures were gaining on them. Damon was a step behind Ashlie, making sure she was all right. They reached the foot of the mountain and found themselves surrounded by trees.

"Keep going," Damon yelled from behind.

Just as they both started running up the mountainside, Damon felt a hand grab his shoulder tightly, so tight it nearly crushed his shoulder.

"Ahhh," Damon yelled.

The force was unbearable. He grabbed the hand and flung it off and was now face-to-face with the creature. Damon was petrified. The creature had a human head, but half of it looked burnt. It had human legs and its hand was massive and mutated. Damon couldn't think.

After a split-second, he kicked it in the stomach, turned, and ran. The creature fell to the ground and let out a terrifying shriek. Five more mutated creatures ran past it, chasing after Damon and Ashlie. Ashlie was now a few paces in front of Damon and still running. She was too scared to look back. Damon caught up with her.

Still not turning around Ashlie asked, "You okay?"

"Yeah, just hurt my shoulder. I think we lost them, though," Damon replied, out of breath.

"Have the creatures gone, can we stop?" Ashlie asked slowing down.

"Yeah, I think so," Damon replied, striding up to her and stopping again.

They both looked back and couldn't see anything in the darkness.

"How is your shoulder?" Ashlie asked.

"My shoulder is okay now, thanks." Damon replied, holding his shoulder as they walked on.

The path they were walking along went up and down, and this tired them even more. The sun was rising and now they could see ahead more clearly.

"What is that?" Ashlie asked, pointing in the distance as they came to a clearing.

Squinting, Damon said, "Is that a spear with a human head on it?"

"Not just one," Ashlie said, pointing to five others.

Grabbing Ashlie's shoulder and looking from left to right at the human heads, Damon replied, "We are definitely a long way from home now! I don't think this place is safe. At all."

"Keep your eyes and ears open, we need to get off this mountain," Damon continued, gently pulling Ashlie towards him.

"Okay, any idea where we are?" Ashlie asked, knowing what his answer would be.

"No, but I know we have to keep moving and find somewhere safe out of these trees."

Ashlie stood still and looked around, then quickly followed him.

In despair, she asked, "Where are we gonna go?"

"I don't know but we have to head north," Damon replied pointing the way.

They came to a hollow in the mountainside where a meteor had struck and left a crater in the ground in front of them.

"Wow, big hole," Ashlie said looking into the crater.

Pointing at it, Damon asked, "Yes, but what's that beyond it?"

"It looks like a village, maybe the people in the village can help us, tell us where we are," Ashlie replied hopefully.

Damon was worried, "I don't know."

But Ashlie had already started walking towards the village.

"Ashlie, wait," Damon called, jogging after her.

He caught up with her, "We have to be careful; we don't know who or what could be in that village. Let me go first."

"Okay, macho man," Ashlie said sarcastically.

Damon ignored her comment and ordered, "If it's dangerous, you have to run, okay?"

"Fine," Ashlie agreed.

They walked cautiously towards the village and could see a stable with two horses, a windmill with a large out-building and five separate smaller houses. Damon walked up to the village with Ashlie behind him. He turned, looked at her and told her to stop then walked into the village. There were two men who immediately walked over to him. Both had large swords strapped across their chests.

In a very croaky voice Damon asked, "Hi, my name is Damon, would you please tell me where I am?"

Instantly both men drew their swords and raised them threateningly. Damon tilted his head back and stood motionless. The men started shouting at Damon in a language he didn't understand. Damon took two steps back and the men took two steps towards him. They shouted at him again, louder this time.

Stepping back Damon asked, "English?"

The men didn't reply.

Damon turned and shouted to Ashlie, "Run!"

As his back was turned one of the men speared him through the leg. Damon fell to his knees and screamed in pain.

The other man struck him on the head, knocking him out. Ashlie gasped, put her hands over her mouth, turned and ran away. The two men ignored her. They picked Damon up by his shoulders and dragged him to one of the houses.

Chapter 3

Return of Silver

Angalie, Jenavieve, Jimmy, and Josh were running as fast as they could to get away from the mutated man. The mutant was stumbling over the gravel, staggering from side to side as it chased after them, screeching at them.

Turning and looking at the mutant, Jenavieve yelled, "It's gaining on us."

"Keep running," Jimmy called, racing past Jenavieve.

Josh looked into the distance and panted, "There's a river up ahead, maybe we can lose it there."

"Yeah, it might be afraid of water," Angalie hoped.

The four of them got to the river and jumped in. They started treading water, holding their bags above their heads. The mutant was only a few metres behind them but came to a halt when it saw the river. It let out a loud screech as it turned and lurched away. The river was deep and the strong current was dragging them downstream. They were holding their heads just above the waterline but still taking in gulps of water.

Jimmy had his head tilted back.

"You guys okay?" he called, holding his bag up above his head.

"Yeah," Jenavieve called back. "We should try to get to the other bank and get out. I don't know how long I can hold my bag and tread water."

Jimmy was breathing heavily and kicking as hard and as fast as he could to stay afloat. They tried to swim to the opposite riverbank but the current was too strong and kept pulling them downstream. After some time, they began to lose their strength. Angalie was first to drop her bag and she started to get cramp in her legs. Moments later she began to sink.

Jimmy was closest to her and saw her go under. He took a deep breath and shouted, "Angalie!"

He dropped his bag and dived down. With all the strength in his body and using the current, Jimmy edged his way towards her. He grabbed her and with one huge kick of his legs, pulled her up to the surface.

Jimmy held on to Angalie, keeping her head above the water. She had passed out.

Jenavieve was farther downstream. She was looking back at them and cried, "Is she okay?"

"Yeah, but she's passed out," Jimmy replied, still holding her head above the water.

"The river is getting shallower and the current weaker over here," Josh shouted as he dragged himself towards the opposite bank of the river holding on to his bag.

Jenavieve used her right hand to hold her bag tightly and with her left arm she dragged herself towards Josh and the riverbank. Jimmy leant back and, holding Angalie, kicked himself through the water towards them. Josh got to the bank first and grabbed hold of a tree branch. He threw his bag up on to the bank. Josh pulled himself out of the river and flopped on to the dry ground. Jenavieve caught up with him and did the same.

"Help me with her," Jimmy shouted as he reached the bank.

Josh grabbed Angalie's shoulder and with Jenavieve's help, pulled her onto the bank. Angalie lay motionless, still unconscious. Jimmy got out of the water and leant over Angalie. He pressed her chest fifteen times then held her nose and blew air into her mouth. He repeated the action, again and again. After a while, Angalie finally heaved and spat out a mouthful of water.

"Are you okay?" Jimmy asked, holding Angalie's head and looking into her eyes.

"Yeah, thank you," Angalie replied slowly, breathing heavily.

"We should carry on to Ville de Parie if you can walk. Or do you need to rest?" Jenavieve asked, picking up her bag.

Slowly getting to her feet Angalie answered, "I'm a little tired but I can walk. Where's my bag, by the way?"

"Gone, down the river with mine," Jimmy replied, pointing downstream.

Looking around, Josh asked, "Any idea which way to go?"

Jenavieve pointed, "It's that way, that's all I know."

She remembered the way from when she'd looked at the map earlier.

"So, the river dragged us in the right direction." Josh said, whilst flinging his bag over his shoulder.

Leading the way, Jenavieve said, "Okay, let's go."

The others followed.

They soon came upon a snow-covered forest. Looking around, the forest appeared uninhabited, but they could hear noises in the distance. It sounded like wolves howling and owls hooting in the trees.

Stepping out of the snow and on to a rock Jenavieve said, "We should get some rest and find a place to sleep before it gets too dark."

"Yeah, good idea," Jimmy agreed, looking for a suitable place.

Angalie asked nervously, "Do you think there are wolves here?"

"I don't know, but over there is a good place to spend the night. There's a lot of shelter," Jimmy replied, pointing to the trees.

They walked over to the spot and sat down. The sun was setting but it was still light.

Jenavieve started to make a fire. "If there are wolves, this should keep them away."

The moon was high in the sky which made it hard to sleep. They lay with their heads on their bags. Suddenly, there were loud howlings coming from every direction.

"What is that?" Angalie asked, as they all sat up fast and looked around.

Squinting, Jenavieve replied, "I don't know, I can't see anything out there."

Josh said, "It sounds like a pack of wolves!"

The howling got louder and louder.

"They're getting closer!" Jimmy said nervously.

The howling stopped as suddenly as it had started and turned into growls and heavy breathing. They could hear light footsteps.

"What are we going to do?" Angalie asked in a whisper, squeezing Jimmy's hand tightly.

"Grab a rock or a hard object to defend yourself with. Stand back to back; if whatever's out there attacks, we have to be ready," Jenavieve said, grabbing Josh and pulling him away. "Jimmy, protect Angalie. Josh and I will be just over here."

Scared, Angalie asked, "How many do you think are out there?"

"I don't know but sounds like a lot more than four," Jimmy replied.

With rocks in their hands, they stood back to back, shaking but ready to defend themselves. All of a sudden, there was a loud yelp and they heard something crash to the ground in the distance.

Angalie heard a squeal; she turned to Jimmy and asked, "What was that?"

Jimmy looked at her and replied, "I don't know, but maybe one of the wolves got hurt."

They stood still and didn't move. They could hear louder growls now and barking in the distance.

"We should go see what's happening out there," Josh said, slowly walking towards the sounds.

Angalie grabbed his arm, stopped him, and said, "Are you crazy?"

"No, he's right," Jenavieve said. "We should go check it out." She walked past them in to the dark. The others followed.

They got to some open ground and in the moonlight, saw what they were afraid of: A pack of wolves, surrounding someone.

"Who's that?" Angalie asked, looking at the person in the distance.

Peering into the darkness, Josh asked, "I can't see; is it a girl?"

"It looks like Silver," Jenavieve said.

The pack of wolves turned and was now facing the four of them, fangs bared, nostrils flaring, and ears back. They were about to attack when the girl ran towards one wolf, jumped, and plunged a sword into its neck. She did a roly-poly and then landed in front of the four.

It was Silver.

"Long time," she said, grinning.

The wolves snarled and then ran off.

"So how have you been?" she asked as if nothing had just happened.

"We've been good," Jimmy said. "How have you been? I thought you were going home? Where are Sam and Raven?"

"I went home and found my parents' bodies. Everything was gone, everyone was dead. There were these mutated creatures that were feasting on all the bodies and many more mutated creatures had made camp there, so I left," Silver explained. She continued, "I ran from them and luckily wound up here. But Sam and Raven weren't so lucky; the creatures killed them. Oh, and to your other question, my parents taught me how to fight with swords when I was younger. I can teach you if you want."

"What else have you come across around here?" Angalie asked Silver anxiously, immediately regretting the question.

"A lot. The mutated creatures were by far the worst thing I've seen. I noticed, though, that they're scared of water and fire. They come in all different shapes and sizes."

They all looked at her intrigued, and Jimmy asked, "What do you mean, 'shapes and sizes'?"

"I noticed that the taller mutated creatures are slower and weaker; they also can't run properly."

Jenavieve, frightened, looked deep into Silver's eyes and asked, "What other types of creatures are there?"

"I call them Screechers. They have sharp teeth. They run on all fours along the ground and are very fast and strong. They make a loud screech which you've probably heard. We can't stay here; it's not safe."

Silver put her swords in her belt and turned and walked away.

"Okay," Jimmy said, picking up a bag and walking after her. The others followed behind.

"I passed a cavern a while back," Silver said, leading the way. "We can stay there tonight and go on in the morning to search for your parents."

After walking for some time, they got to the cavern and sat down. The floor of the cavern was frozen over; it was very cold.

"It's freezing in here," Josh said, rubbing his arms vigorously to warm himself up.

"I'll gather some branches and try to make a fire. Stop complaining," Silver barked at Josh.

Jimmy walked out of the frozen cavern with Silver. The ground was covered in snow.

"I'll help you," he said. "Not many branches around."

"We may have to go a bit farther to find any branches," she replied, smiling at him.

Back at the cavern, the others were sitting in a circle on their bags. They were rubbing their shoulders and chests to warm themselves.

"They've been gone a long time," Angalie remarked.

"Yeah, do you think they're okay?" Josh asked.

"I'm sure they're fine, plus Silver has her swords on her," Jenavieve replied.

Jimmy and Silver came to a clearing. "Finally, some branches," Jimmy called to Silver.

Silver turned, looked at Jimmy, and froze.

Staring at him she whispered, "Jimmy, don't move!"

Chapter 4

Separate

Ashlie made it to the crater and looked back at the village. She saw a man put his foot into the stirrup and pull himself up to mount his horse. He started trotting away. She kept staring at the village where Damon had been taken. She sighed to herself, then turned and strode away.

Back at the village, the two men dragged Damon into one of the houses and chained him to the wall. Damon stood, weak and barely conscious, in the crucifix position. His head was on his chest, and the chains were tight around each wrist. When he regained full consciousness, he groaned, pulled on the chains, and shouted, "What are you doing to me?"

The two men were chatting in a foreign language. They stood up and walked over to him, and one yelled at him in a deep tone, "*Oins, gloshca copa.*"

"What? I don't speak your stupid language," Damon said, frustrated, exhausted and breathing heavily. He felt like a ragdoll in chains.

"*Oins, gloshca copa?*" the man said again.

Bobbing his head from left to right, Damon replied, "I don't understand what that means."

The man stepped forward, smacked Damon across the face, and said again, "*Oins, gloshca copa?*"

Damon's head fell to the left, and he spat out a mouthful of blood. He raised his head again and looked at the two men straight in the face, blood and saliva dripping from his mouth.

"Who are you? Why are you doing this to me?" Damon groaned in a whisper; his eyes closed, and he was out of breath.

The second man walked forward, grabbed Damon's shoulder, and punched him hard in the stomach. Damon gasped, "Ugh." He threw his head back and then forward, still chained in the crucifix position.

"*Oins, gloshca copa?*" the man shouted at him again.

Damon took half a step, tilted his head, and just stared at the man. He groaned again, lowered his head, and looked at the ground. The two men spoke to each other and then left.

Watching them walk out, Damon called, "Hey, where are you going?"

They shut the door behind them.

He closed his eyes and started thinking about Ashlie; he had to escape. A while later, the two men came back into the room, accompanied by another man and a woman. They all spoke together, and then the two men left. The third man was holding a bag.

Damon thought the worst; he thought he was about to be tortured by these two. He shook nervously, petrified of what was going to happen.

The woman spoke in English, saying in an accent, "No need to be afraid, we are not going to hurt you."

Damon just stood still, looking at her. She reached up and unlocked the chains. Damon fell to the ground. The woman picked him up with one hand on his back and walked him over to a table in the corner; she helped him lay down.

"This man will heal your wound," she said to Damon in a soothing voice, looking at the other man. "He is our doctor; he will treat your leg."

Damon's voice shook with fear as he said quietly, "Thank you."

He lay back and closed his eyes whilst the doctor examined his leg.

"Sorry about what those men did to you," the woman said, sitting on the table next to Damon's head. "Those were not my orders."

Damon opened his eyes and repeated, "Your orders?"

"Yes," the woman replied. "My orders were that any humans were to be brought straight to me,"

"Who are you? And what language were they talking in?"

She answered, "My name is Coralie. We are from a place far away. Our town was overrun by the mutants; it was impossible to defend, so we fled. I am the commander; we rebuilt our town here the best we could. Many of us took shelter in the old castle. It gave us a clear view of the landscape so we could see when the mutated men were coming. I taught my villagers how to defend themselves. We are a fighter race; we've had to be, as we faced many invaders in the past. I know many different languages such as yours. My men harmed you because they thought you were one of the mutants."

"What do you plan to do with me once I have healed?" Damon asked anxiously.

"That depends on you," Coralie replied. "If you answer my questions, nothing will happen. If you don't, well, you don't want to find out."

"Um, okay, what do you want to know?" Damon asked tensely.

"The same one the two men were asking you earlier: '*Oins, gloshca copa.*' This means, how many of you are there? How many people do you have?"

"What? How many people do I have for what?" Damon asked, not understanding what she meant.

"Wrong answer," Coralie said, nodding to the doctor.

The doctor had strapped up Damon's leg and placed chains on Damon's wrists. He dragged Damon back over to the wall and attached the chains to the ceiling, lifting him off the ground, hanging the prisoner by his wrists.

Damon cried, "Stop. Don't do this. I don't know anything or how many people we have or what that even means."

Coralie slowly walked over to Damon and ripped off his shirt; she threw it on the floor, took a knife out of her pocket, and said, "This can be very painful or quick and easy, up to you; just tell me what I want to know."

"I'm telling you the truth. You think I want to get hurt? If I knew anything, I'd tell you," Damon said, twisting and turning like a fish out of water.

"That's not what I want to hear," Coralie replied as she slowly ran the knife down Damon's chest and watched the blood drip down his stomach onto his shorts.

"Okay, okay, okay, just stop. I'll tell you whatever you want to know," Damon said, clenching his jaw and squeezing his eyes shut tightly.

"Finally, we're getting somewhere. That wasn't so hard, was it?" Coralie asked, putting the knife back in her pocket.

"No," Damon replied, irritated.

"So, how many?" Coralie asked, getting annoyed.

"Okay, well, you know the meteors hit our towns and villages, so hundreds were killed. I know that there were many survivors, about two hundred," Damon said quickly. Hoping it would be enough information.

"I already know about the meteors. Only two hundred? That's interesting. I hope you're not lying to me," Coralie replied as she removed the chains.

Damon again fell to his knees. He grabbed his shirt, wincing in pain as he put it back on, and asked, "What now?"

"You will stay here for now," Coralie replied. "It's not safe in the woods. The mutants are still out there. I've sent a man to see if your claims are true. If not, well, that won't be good for you."

Damon slowly got up and asked, "Okay, and the friend I was traveling with, what about her?"

"Oh, the girl? I think she is long gone, especially with the mutants lurking around. The doctor will take you to a room. You can spend the night there." Coralie turned and walked out.

Damon got to the room and saw that the only thing in there was a bed. He sat on the edge of the bed, thinking about Ashlie. He lay back, took a deep breath, and tried to get some sleep.

***

Ashlie walked nervously through the forest. She looked left and right. All around her were trees, and the crater was behind her. She continued walking deeper into the forest, knowing that she'd have to stop soon and find somewhere to rest. The temperature had dropped; she rubbed her arms to keep warm. Darkness fell; suddenly, there were sounds coming from every direction.

The sounds seemed to be getting closer. She sped up her pace to a light jog, trying to get out of the forest. As she jogged, she sensed something behind her, stalking her. She thought to herself, *"Could the man from the village have caught up with me? Probably not. It would have to be something else."* She didn't like the thought that it might be something else.

Hearing twigs snapping behind her, she broke into a run. It was hard going because the ground was rising. Her heart was racing. She could feel a real chill in the air but kept going. She took a quick look back and couldn't see anything behind her. She slowed to jog again, her knees trembling as she ran. She thought she could see a field in the distance ahead; looking back one last time to make sure she wasn't being followed, she ran towards it. She stopped at a tree just before the field and gazed out.

It was dark, but she could make out some figures in the field. There were dead deer on the ground, which were being feasted on by what looked like people. The people were on all fours; they had ripped out the deer's throats, blood all over their faces. One looked up and saw Ashlie. She gasped and quickly covered her mouth.

"They're not human, they're mutants," she thought to herself.

The mutant didn't get up from the ground but slowly crawled towards her. Ashlie took a slow step backward, staring straight at the crawling mutant as it let out a deafening, high-pitched screech. The other mutants stopped feasting and looked up at Ashlie.

Her legs shook, and she stumbled and fell. All the mutants began crawling towards her; they were all glowering. The one closest to her had a mutated head and giant hands. The two behind him had skin like sandpaper. The two at the back had mutated arms with huge fingers; their legs were disjointed, and their heads were burnt and bruised.

Ashlie jumped up and ran back into the forest as fast as she could, not looking back at them. All five let out a deafening screech and then began chasing after her. Ashlie bobbed and weaved in between the trees, trying to lose them but they ran on all fours like dogs and quickly gained on her. They were right behind her, within touching distance. Ashlie jumped to avoid the first mutant's hand. She was getting tired and didn't think she could keep up this pace for much longer.

In the distance, she saw the crater, and beyond that was the villager who had been sent to find her. She thought that if she could reach him, she might be safe.

As she sprinted up to the crater, two of the mutants screeched and tried to grab her arms. Ashlie could see them in her peripheral vision as she leapt into the crater. The two mutants just missed her arms and stopped at the edge of the crater, screeching again.

Ashlie rolled head over heels down into the crater, rolling over and over as she fell. She hit the bottom with a hard crash. Groaning, she looked up at them.

The man from the village was on the far side of the crater. He stared down at Ashlie and then towards the mutants with a worried look on his face. The mutants let out another screech and ran around the rim of the crater. They were upon the villager in seconds; before he had time to get away. They grabbed him and started biting chunks of flesh out of his neck. Ashlie saw that they were no longer interested in her, so she quietly climbed out of the crater and ran off.

It started to rain, but she didn't care; she was hot but knew she had to get away from the area. The rain had made the ground muddy; she was slipping and sliding as she ran. She was so tired; she couldn't go any farther. She found a place to rest in amongst some trees; she hastily made a fire. She sat up against a tree, put her head in her hands, and started crying. There was no way she could sleep, knowing what was out there.

Just then, she heard footsteps in the distance; petrified, she snatched up a sharp stone, took a deep breath, and stood up, ready to fight as several figures came into view.

She couldn't believe what she saw.

Chapter 5

Escape

"What is it?" Jimmy asked, looking at Silver.

"On your left," she said quietly.

Jimmy turned slowly and saw a group of Screechers, leering at him, saliva dripping from their mouths. Jimmy stood in shock, unable to move. The Screechers let out a long shriek. Jimmy was terrified. Silver rushed over to him and handed him a sword.

She said, "Take this to defend yourself with. We have to go."

Jimmy and Silver ran off, and the Screechers chased after them.

"They're faster than us," Jimmy yelled as they ran.

"Yeah, I think we're gonna have to fight," Silver said. "Remember the fighting techniques Roan taught you at the training camp? You'll need to use them."

They neared the cavern where Josh, Jenavieve, and Angalie were.

Jimmy and Silver stopped and turned to face the Screechers. One of them jumped at Jimmy, baring its teeth. It aimed straight for his throat. With his sword, Jimmy hacked at the Screecher's face, knocking it to the side. Instantly, another one jumped and knocked Jimmy to the ground. Jimmy protected his face with his hands.

At the same time, two other Screechers were circling Silver. One sprang at her; she ran her sword through its stomach and threw it aside, just like Roan had taught her. The second Screecher saw what happened and leaped towards her, screeching loudly. Silver spun when she heard the noise, grabbed it by the shoulder, and slit its throat.

Jimmy was still on the ground, fighting the Screecher on top of him. She dashed over and stabbed it through the skull. Blood gushed onto Jimmy's face. He pushed it aside and wiped away the blood as Silver helped him up.

"That was easier than I thought," Silver said as she stepped over to the last Screecher and skewered it through the heart.

"I guess our training paid off," Jimmy said, looking at his blood covered hands.

"Yeah, it did."

She noticed Jimmy's hands and added, "We're gonna have to get that stitched up."

"Yeah, that cut is pretty deep."

Just then, they heard the trees rustling behind them.

"What's that?" Jimmy asked nervously as they both turned and saw dozens of figures in the distance. "That's a lot of mutants."

"We can't take them all," Silver said as they slowly walked backward away from them. When they got close to the cavern, Jimmy called in, "Josh, Jenavieve, Angalie: get out of there and head for Ville de Parie. Silver and I will try and buy you some time to get away."

"No, we are not leaving you," Angalie shouted.

"There are too many. Go home and find your parents," Silver yelled back.

As the mutants came into view, Josh, Jenavieve, and Angalie realised that there were too many. They didn't have weapons, so they knew that even with their training there was little they could do.

Jimmy whispered to Silver, "We can't fight them; we will die. I think we can just lead them away. These are the slow mutants, right?"

"Yeah, that's right," Silver whispered, staring at the mutants as they edged closer.

Jimmy pointed and hissed, "That way, through those trees." He grabbed Silver's arm and ran towards the trees, making sure that the mutants had seen them and were following them.

Jenavieve saw the mutants run after Jimmy and Silver.

"C'mon, this way is safe; let's go. Follow me." she said to Josh and Angalie.

They headed towards the mountain, unhappy about leaving Silver and Jimmy behind.

"I hope they will be okay," Angalie said as she followed Josh and Jenavieve.

Looking at the map to remind herself of the way, Jenavieve said, "Keep your eyes open; we don't know what else is out there."

They walked for hours in the direction of Ville de Parie. They were tired and needed to rest.

Pointing to a grassy clearing, Josh said, "I'm exhausted. Let's stop over there."

They walked over and sat down. Instinctively, Jenavieve started to gather wood for a fire, "This should keep us warm for the night."

After the fire was lit, Angalie asked, "How far do you think it is to Ville de Parie?"

"Not sure," Josh replied, "but I'm guessing it's pretty far."

Jenavieve said, "I'm gonna try to make spears from saplings so we have something to protect ourselves with, okay?"

At the training camp, Roan had taught them how to pick the right sort of saplings to make good spears and how to sharpen one end for impaling. Jenavieve had enjoyed this part of the training the most and was the best at it.

"Okay, good idea," Angalie replied, lying on her back and trying to get comfortable.

After Jenavieve finished making three spears, she handed one to each of them.

"Nice," Josh said as he swung the spear around.

"Thanks," Angalie said as she jabbed the air above her, still lying on her back.

"We'll head out at first light," Jenavieve said, as she laid her spear next to her and tried to get some rest.

"All right," Josh and Angalie said in agreement.

***

Jimmy and Silver ran as fast as they could through the trees, with the mutants chasing them. The mutants ran slowly, and their vision wasn't good, but they had a good sense of smell. Jimmy's hands were still bleeding; his blood was dripping on the ground, so the mutants were able to track him easily.

Silver stopped at a tree and bent over to catch her breath whilst Jimmy caught up with her. She said, "I think we're in the clear for now."

He looked back and couldn't see them, but just then, they came out of the trees and let out a huge screech as they kept walking towards Jimmy and Silver.

"What? How did they find us?" Silver asked, still breathing heavily. She gazed at Jimmy's hands and said, "Your hands; they can smell the blood from your hands."

Jimmy looked at his bloody hands. He wiped the blood on the bottom of his shirt, tore the bloody piece off, and dropped it on the ground, saying, "C'mon, we have to keep moving."

Still out of breath, Silver nodded and followed him. The mutants stopped at the torn piece of shirt. One of them picked it up and smelt it. The mutants roared and carried on walking after Jimmy and Silver. This distraction bought Jimmy and Silver time to get away.

"I think we lost them," Jimmy said after a while, looking back.

Silver turned and said, "Yeah, but I don't think that's the last we'll see of them."

"Yeah," Jimmy replied, slowing down to save his energy.

They carried on. It was dark and cold, so Jimmy rubbed his chest to keep warm.

"We need to rest," Silver said, her heart still pounding.

"Yeah, all right," Jimmy replied, looking back one last time. He thought he saw something. He took a couple of steps and squinted.

"What is it?" Silver asked.

"What's that in the distance?"

"I don't know; it's not them again, is it?"

"If it is, we won't have much time to rest," Jimmy said.

Silver replied, "Yeah, let's go; it will take time for them to reach us."

Tired and annoyed, they carried on walking. They came to a narrow river and stopped. A wild boar was drinking. To its left were some mutated deer, also drinking. The animals ignored each other.

"What should we do?" Silver asked, watching the animals.

"Well, I think we have to cross the river," Jimmy said. "The mutants won't cross it, so we'll be safe on the other side."

One of the deer heard them talking and looked up. Its head was mutated, with a second head growing out of it.

"Eww, that's gross," Silver said, staring at the deer. The deer stared back then ran; spooking the rest of the deer.

Meanwhile, the wild boar kept drinking.

They watched the deer leave and turned to look at the wild boar. They waited for it to finish drinking and leave so they could cross the river.

"It's taking forever," Silver said, still staring at the boar.

"Maybe it didn't hear us," Jimmy suggested.

Silver picked up a small stone, tossed it up and down, and then chucked it at the wild boar. She hit it straight on the back.

"Why did you do that?" Jimmy snapped angrily.

"We need to cross, and it's taking too long," Silver replied.

The wild boar snorted at them. It was very muscular, with huge tusks and lots of sharp, jagged teeth. The boar pawed the dirt with its hoof as it prepared to charge.

"He looks mad," Silver said.

Jimmy grabbed his sword, ready to fight, and Silver did the same.

"Any ideas?" Jimmy asked.

"Don't die."

The wild boar charged. In a blink, it was upon them. Attacking Silver, it leapt straight at her. Swinging its head, its tusk gored her in the stomach, sending her flying backward.

It then turned towards Jimmy, who gripped his sword tightly with both hands. The wild boar charged at his legs. Jimmy leapt into the air to avoid contact, but the wild boar rammed his leg, gouging it. From above, Jimmy plunged the sword into the wild boar's shoulder as they both crashed to the ground.

The boar tossed and turned with the sword in its shoulder, trying to get it out. Silver lay on the ground, holding her stomach and groaning. But she saw an opportunity to kill the boar. She grabbed her sword, limped over to the wild boar, and waited for it to stop moving. Then, she stabbed it through the throat.

The wild boar was dead. Silver pulled her sword out and cleaned it. Jimmy hobbled over to the boar and pulled his sword out of its shoulder.

"You okay?" he asked Silver, who was holding her stomach.

"I'll be fine. How's your leg?" Silver asked, looking at the cut.

"It's just a scratch," Jimmy said. "I'll be fine. How is your stomach?"

Silver, holding her stomach in pain, said, "It wasn't that deep, so it should be all right."

"Okay, good. Can you walk?" Jimmy asked.

She replied, "Yeah," as she grabbed Jimmy's shoulder, and they walked over to the river.

They knelt by the river and put their hands in to see how cold the water was.

"Not too bad," Jimmy said, getting to his feet and helping Silver up.

The mutants were close now. They could hear them.

"We have to jump in," Silver said, looking at Jimmy and then pointing behind at the approaching mutants.

"Yeah," Jimmy said. "On three: one … two … three." They held hands and jumped in.

The current dragged them downstream. Jimmy shouted above the noise of the river, "Try to stay afloat until it gets shallow."

The mutants arrived at the riverbank and screeched at them in anger; they didn't dare enter the water. Due to their mutation, their bone density was too high, and they couldn't float.

"Okay," Silver said, doing breaststroke with her free arm and trying to keep her head above the water.

The current weakened as they swam downstream.

"Can you make it to the bank?" Jimmy asked, still holding Silver's hand tightly.

"Yeah," Silver shouted using one arm and kicking herself to the bank.

They got to the bank and pulled themselves out. Jimmy helped Silver up and asked, "How's your stomach now?"

"It's okay. I'm just a bit tired, that's all," Silver replied, holding on to Jimmy's shoulder and breathing heavily. "What's that?" she asked, nodding towards the forest in the distance.

Jimmy turned to see and replied, "Looks like smoke."

"Let's go see."

As they walked through the trees, a girl appeared, holding a stone in her hand, ready to fight.

Staring at the girl in front of them, Jimmy exclaimed, "Who's that!"

Chapter 6

Dungeons

Damon woke to a banging on the door. He slowly got up and opened it.

Coralie was standing in front of him, with two guards behind her. She said, "I brought you some breakfast."

"Thanks," Damon replied, as he looked down and took the tray from her.

"My two scouts haven't returned yet, and there's no sign of your friend," she said. "Sorry."

Damon looked at her, upset.

"Eat your breakfast, then I'll show you around the village," Coralie said, turning and walking away with her guards.

Damon moved back to the bed and ate the food. The room he had slept in had no furniture other than the bed. After he had finished eating, he got up and went outside. Not waiting for Coralie, he walked into the centre of the village. There were four houses there. He looked through a window into one of them and could see that it was full of weapons. Walking to the next house, he saw it had only one room. It was full of animal carcasses, hanging from the ceiling; they dripped blood onto the floor. A wood fire was burning in the room. He looked over at the other two houses on the far side. From where he stood, he could see that they were the same as the room he had slept in, just one bed against the back wall. There were no people around in the village. He started wondering what was going on and where Coralie had gone.

Damon continued walking. He passed a couple of trees and then saw a stable with two brown horses tied up outside. Other horses were resting inside the stable. Damon ignored them and carried on. In the distance, he could see a large castle. It was surrounded by many smaller houses. He strode towards the castle. Four guards, wearing helmets and holding large spears, immediately marched up to him and stopped right in front of him. Damon took two steps back. He took a big slow breath to ease his fear.

At that moment, Coralie appeared out of the castle and walked over to the guards. She touched one of them on the shoulder, and they parted.

She said, "Glad you found me. I'll show you around."

"Okay," Damon said, knowing he didn't have much say in the matter.

"This way." Coralie put her arm on Damon's shoulder and pushed him forward.

He said nervously, "I saw the village already."

"Okay, I'll show you the main quarters," Coralie said, grinning. "Relax; there's no need to be nervous."

Damon said, "Okay," but he was still nervous.

As they walked, Coralie pointed out what each house represented.

Looking at the castle, Damon asked, "Is that where you live?"

"Yeah, you want to go inside?"

He smiled and said, "Sure."

In the first room, inside the castle, there was a large table in the centre with a seat at the back. To the left of the table was another room closed off by a curtain. The walls were made of white stone, and there were long windows on both sides with broken glass.

Damon looked through the curtain into the second room and saw a young girl in chains; she was covered with blisters, and he could see what looked like injection marks all over her body. She looked mutated.

Startled by what he saw, Damon asked, "Is that your room?" pointing towards the curtained-off area.

"Yeah, that's my room," Coralie replied, "and this is where we have our council meetings," she continued, gesturing at the table whilst turning him away from the room.

With a quick look back at Coralie's room, Damon asked, "Was that a mutant in your room?"

She replied, "I wish you hadn't seen that."

She explained to Damon that the mutated girl he had seen was her little sister; she needed fresh virus-free blood in order to live. This was why the dungeons were full of people.

They heard noises coming from outside. A man walked in with two guards behind him. He spoke in Coralie's language and said, "*Le noud sih elope, ret from nat eh dais.*"

Damon stared blankly and asked, "What did he say?"

She replied, "He said that he found your people and that there were more of them than you let on."

"What? How about Ashlie?"

Coralie ignored him.

"*Eseze meh,*" she said to the guards.

The two guards walked over to Damon and grabbed him.

Petrified, Damon asked, "Wait! What are you doing?"

He tried to shake the men off as Coralie snapped, "You shouldn't have lied to me."

"*Nihach meh, tup meh ni het snegund,*" she commanded the guards.

As the men dragged him out of the castle, Damon yelled, "Where are you taking me?"

"To the dungeons."

The guards marched Damon through the village to some steps which led down to a tunnel. The two guards started striding through the tunnel, dragging Damon with them; Coralie close behind. The tunnel was lit with pine torches. Damon looked around at the tunnel walls. There were markings on the walls that he had never seen before. As they got to the end of the tunnel, Coralie passed them and opened a huge wooden door with a bronze key.

The guards trooped Damon in. The large room was dark, even though it was lit with four torches, one in each corner. The guards pushed Damon over to one side of the room; they chained his legs together and to the wall, and then they left. After Damon's eyes adjusted to the dark, he saw that other people were lying on the ground, also chained up. He thought they were dead but decided to ask, "Hey, do you speak English?"

There was no reply; Damon just sat looking at the figures in the dark. Eventually, one of them sat up and said in a gravelly voice, "Yeah, we speak English."

Damon felt a surge of relief and asked, "What are your names?"

The figure sitting up replied, "I am Bellomie; next to me is my sister Rosalie, and next to her is King, who came in shortly after us."

"Who is that over there in the corner?" Damon asked.

"'That was Julien,' Bellomie replied. "He was with Rosalie and me, but they killed him to make us cooperate and then just left him there."

"How long have you been here?" Damon asked.

"I don't know; maybe two, three days now. We got captured running from the mutants."

Pulling on the chain around his ankle to see if he could get loose, Damon asked, "Did they give you any food or water?"

"Yeah, they did, but it's like they're preparing us for something bad!" Bellomie replied. He watched Damon try to free himself and then said, "You can't escape; we tried."

"Thanks," Damon said, sitting back against the wall and looking angrily at the chains.

King and Rosalie sat up at the same time; Rosalie said, "Oh, great; they got another one."

"Yeah, he's Damon," Bellomie said.

"Hi," Damon said.

"Hi," Rosalie replied, looking at Damon's dark figure. "What do you think they want with us? Why keep us here?"

"Don't know," Damon replied.

Damon knew what was going to happen but didn't want to say anything to them.

Moments later, a guard entered the dungeon with a tray, put down dishes of food and water, and said in a deep voice, "Eat, drink."

"I guess we should 'Eat, drink,'" Damon said, mocking the guard.

"Yeah," Rosalie replied with a chuckle.

They ate their food, drank the water, and waited.

"This is driving me crazy, just waiting, wondering what they're going to do to us," Bellomie said to no one in particular.

"Yeah, me too," King replied, wiping the food from his mouth.

The four of them sat against the walls, staring hopelessly into space.

***

Ashlie dropped her stone and said, "Oh, my God; it's so good to see people."

Silver and Jimmy hobbled over to her, smiling, and asked, "What's your name?"

"Ashlie," she replied.

"Are you alone out here?" Silver asked.

"I wasn't earlier. I was running from those mutated things, but they got distracted, and I got away," Ashlie replied, her heart racing in her chest.

Confused, Silver asked, "Distracted?"

"Yeah, I was with my friend Damon. We went into this village, looking for somewhere safe to spend the night, but some men attacked Damon. He told me to run. That's when I came across the mutants. I'm guessing the village sent a man after me, and the mutants decided to kill him instead of me."

"So, was your friend Damon captured?" Jimmy asked.

"Yeah."

Staring at both of them, Silver asked, "Okay, so what's the plan now? We can't stay here, in case the mutants come back."

"I don't know. You're injured and so am I," Jimmy said, looking at Silver.

Silver thought about this.

"I think I should try to rescue Damon," Ashlie said. "I could really use your help."

"All right," Jimmy said, "but after we get some rest."

"Okay, we'll rest and then go," Silver said. "Just one thing: were the mutants standing up, or were they on all fours?'

"They ran on all fours," Ashlie answered.

"Those aren't mutated men; they're Screechers," Silver explained. "They're a lot worse than mutated men, faster and stronger."

Ashlie's jaw dropped.

Jimmy pointed at Silver's stomach and said, "Let me see your wound."

"I told you, it's not that bad," she replied, lifting her shirt to uncover the wound.

"Ugh," Ashlie said, looking at her stomach.

Jimmy walked over to Silver, felt the wound, and said, "Looks like the river cleaned most of it up; just need to seal it, and it should be fine."

"And your leg?" Silver asked.

"It's also fine," Jimmy replied, showing Silver the cut.

"If you heat your swords in the fire, you can seal your wounds and then we can go," Ashlie said.

"Okay," Silver agreed.

They heated their swords, and Jimmy placed his sword on Silver's wound to cauterise it. Silver put her hand over her mouth to muffle her scream.

"Ouch," she said sarcastically once it was done.

Jimmy stuck his leg out and said, "Okay, I'm ready."

Silver took her sword out of the fire and placed it on his cut, searing the flesh. He put on a brave face and didn't say anything. Jimmy kicked his leg, stretching it, blew out a breath, clenched his fist, and then said, "That hurt a wee little bit."

"You guys okay?" Ashlie asked, looking at them and their wounds.

"Yeah, let's go," Silver ordered, leading the way.

They both followed her.

Walking through the forest, Ashlie took over the lead because she knew the way back to the village. They got to the edge of the forest and found the crater.

Ashlie pointed and said, "Over there is the village where they took Damon. I watched as they dragged him into one of those houses."

"Okay, what's the plan?" Silver asked. "We can't just walk straight into the village. The guards will see us."

"We have to find another way around and try to sneak in," Ashlie suggested.

"Yeah, let's see if there's another way around," Jimmy said. He pointed towards some trees in the distance and continued, "Those should keep us hidden."

The three of them crouched as they walked through the trees, hoping not to be seen. They got to the top of a little hill and looked down on the village. They could see the whole village, plus the castle and all the houses around it.

Irritated, Ashlie said, "Oh, great, he could be in any one of those houses or even the castle."

"If he is a prisoner, I doubt he's in the main castle. We need to find the dungeons," Silver said. "That's most likely where he's being held."

Pointing towards the village, Jimmy asked, "Wait, what's that over there?"

"I don't know," Silver said. "It's too far to see; let's get closer." She began to trot over to the village.

"Silver, wait," Jimmy said, rushing after her.

They were in a clearing at the top of the hill. Jimmy grabbed Silver's hand. They stopped and looked. At the bottom of the hill, a group of villagers were standing in battle formation. A small woman stood in front of them. She was shouting. Every time she shouted at them, they cheered back at her.

Ashlie caught up with them and asked, "Who's that?"

"I don't know, but it looks like she's their leader," Silver replied.

"That's a lot of people," Jimmy said, not taking his eyes off the group.

"Yup," Ashlie replied, still staring.

Silver suggested, "If the villagers are over there, your friend Damon is probably in a dungeon somewhere. He may not be guarded!"

Chapter 7

Mysterious Fog

*I*n the grassy clearing, Jenavieve, Josh, and Angalie woke up with the sun shining on their faces. Jenavieve stretched, studied the map, and looked at Josh and Angalie. She said, "Ready to go?"

Angalie asked, "Do you know which way to go?"

"Yeah, this way," Jenavieve replied, grabbing her spear and pointing with it.

"Okay, let's go," Josh said. He jumped to his feet with his spear in his hand.

Leading them through the woods as they started off on their trek, Jenavieve said, "Be alert. Shout if you see anything."

"Okay, will do," Angalie replied.

There were trees every way they looked; the air was cool, and the sun shone brightly, giving them a clear view of the countryside. Birds were singing in the trees.

"This way," Jenavieve said, speeding up her walk to a light jog.

Josh and Angalie followed suit.

They had jogged for a long time and the sky was starting to cloud over, blocking the sunlight. A dark rain cloud appeared above them.

"Where did that come from?" Josh asked, looking up at the cloud.

"No idea," Angalie replied, following his gaze.

"Just ignore it," Jenavieve called back to them. "We have to keep going."

Angalie and Josh increased their pace and caught up with Jenavieve just as it started to rain.

Covering his head with his hand and spear, Josh said, "That's annoying."

"Let's get to those trees," Angalie suggested, pointing to some oak trees. "They'll provide some cover."

"Yeah, good idea," Josh replied, running to them.

Suddenly, out of nowhere, a wall of fog formed and it was heading towards them.

Josh said, "That's not good."

"No, it's not," Jenavieve said. "That's gonna make things very hard to see."

"What's the plan?" Angalie asked; the fog was now all around them.

"Let's keep going," Jenavieve responded. "We can just walk through the fog."

The fog was so thick that Jenavieve vanished right in front of Josh and Angalie's eyes.

"Take my hand so we don't get separated," Josh said, grabbing Angalie's hand and walking into the fog.

Angalie yelled, "I can't see anything, it's so thick."

"I'm right here and Jenavieve is right in front of me."

They continued, but then from the front, Jenavieve shouted out, "Ahhh," and then was silent.

Josh and Angalie stopped instantly.

"What happened?" Angalie asked, stepping up next to Josh, still holding his hand.

"I don't know."

"Jenavieve!" Josh called out, but there was no reply.

Angalie was worried. She clenched Josh's hand tightly and asked, "Do you think she's okay?"

Josh didn't answer. He was scared.

They stood still, and Angalie yelled, "Jenavieve!"

There was still no answer.

The fog began to clear as fast as it had arrived. Now they could see what had happened. Right in front of them was a crater. Jenavieve had fallen into it and seemed to be unconscious.

"It's so steep," Angalie said. "How're we going to get down there?"

"We'll have to just slide down it," Josh replied, peering into the crater.

"Okay, on three," Angalie replied. "One … two … three." They slid down, sliding past jagged rocks.

They got to the bottom and came to a stop next to Jenavieve. Her head was bleeding. Josh held her head in his hand and wiped the blood, gently shaking her to rouse her.

"Ahhh," she finally said, sitting up and rubbing her head.

"How are you feeling?" Angalie asked, holding her hand.

"I've felt better," Jenavieve replied, trying to smile.

"Can you walk?" Josh asked, helping her up.

"Yeah, I should be able to," she replied. "It's just a bump on the head."

She shook her head and scrambled out of the crater, followed by Angalie and Josh.

"Wait, I recognise these woods. We're nearly home." Jenavieve said happily.

"Really?" Angalie asked.

"Yeah," Jenavieve said as she walked swiftly away. "Follow me."

They came to the edge of the wood and saw that the meteors had destroyed their home; there were craters all over the landscape.

Angalie leant against a tree and whispered sadly to herself, "There's no one here."

Chapter 8

Guinea Pigs

*I*n the dark dungeon, Damon stood up and said, "I can hear something outside." The other three were too far away to hear anything.

"What is it?" Bellomie asked eagerly.

"I can't make it out. I think they're just talking to each other," Damon replied, closing his eyes and trying to focus.

"Can you hear anything now?" King called from the back of the dungeon.

"Wait, I think they're coming in," Damon replied, stepping back against the wall.

The other three stood up, their chains clanking together and echoing throughout the dungeon. They fell silent. Four huge men walked in; each wore a skull mask to cover his face. They held two swords across their chests. The first man walked over to King, sat him down, and undid the chains around his ankles. The other three men stood guard.

"What are you doing? Where are you taking him?" Damon asked as the first man grabbed King's shoulder and pushed him out the door.

Without replying, the men followed King out. Once outside the cell, the guards put a bag over King's head.

"Where are you taking me?" King yelled as the men dragged him through the tunnel.

They walked for what seemed like ages; King had no idea where he was going.

Suddenly, he smelled something and cried, "What is that? It's disgusting. It smells like a sewer."

They came to some stairs; he tripped on the first step and yelled, "Ouch!"

The men dragged him up the stairs. The smell had dissipated, and King could breathe better now. The men stopped at the top and took the bag off his head. Coralie stood in front of him.

King asked, "Why are you doing this?"

Coralie thought about how her parents had been mutated and how she had to kill them. She blamed everyone else for the death of her parents. She stared at King.

Ignoring his question, she said, "I'm going to use you and your friends as guinea pigs to find a cure for my sister. If you can't provide what she needs, then I will find your families and use their blood to make the cure."

King couldn't believe what he was hearing. He thought about his friends and his family, and then he concentrated on the matter at hand: his own survival.

Coralie ordered the guards, "Take him to the doctor."

Fearing for his life, King was led to the doctor's clinic. Coralie followed right behind. Inside, there were ten beds with huge blood taking machines next to them; a syringe was attached at one end of each machine. When King saw this, he took a step back, and his legs turned to jelly. He spotted scalpels and other medical instruments on a table. This made his stomach turn. He looked for a way to escape, but there was none.

"Take him to that bed," she told the guards.

The guards strapped King to the bed; he thrashed about, trying to get loose, but it was hopeless. He continued but was running out of steam. One of the guards had had enough; he strapped King's head down so he couldn't move. King was petrified as he saw the doctor walk towards one of the machines.

"Please don't do this," he begged as the doctor tapped on King's neck to find a vein.

King screamed in pain as the doctor inserted the long syringe. Blood was sucked out of his neck into the machine. Within seconds, King passed out from the pain.

Chapter 9

Rescue

"C'mon, this way," Silver called as she rushed down the hill through the trees.

Jimmy and Ashlie followed, trying to keep up.

From behind, Jimmy called, "Silver, slow down."

Catching up with Silver, the three of them stood together near the bottom of the hill. They were still surrounded by trees.

"We know where the people from the village are," Silver said, "so if we stay away from them, we can make it into the village safely."

Ashlie replied, "Okay, but we should be careful in case some of them stayed behind."

"Good idea," Silver agreed.

Jimmy led the way, saying, "Let's go this way. There's no one around. I think I see the entrance to the village."

"Can we just walk in?" Ashlie asked.

Jimmy drew his sword and said to Silver, "Get your weapon out, just in case."

"Stay in the shadows," Silver said as they walked slowly towards the village.

With their eyes peeled, the three of them came to the first house; they edged along the wall and peered into the village.

Ashlie asked, "I know we just saw the villagers outside but I'm surprised there are no guards around."

Jimmy said, "Yeah, the village seems deserted."

"Let's go on," Silver said, creeping farther into the village.

Jimmy and Ashlie followed; he asked, "Any idea where Damon could be?"

"No idea," Ashlie replied. "He could be anywhere. Why don't we check each house?"

Pointing at the farthest house, Jimmy replied, "Yeah, good idea. I'll check that one."

"I'll check this one, and Ashlie, you check those two, okay?" Silver said, walking away.

Silver went to the house, looked in through the window, and saw it was full of meat. She sighed and turned back to where the others had been standing. Ashlie got to the next house and looked in through the window. There was a bed, but she couldn't see anyone inside, so she walked up to the door and opened it. She was nervous but kept her cool. She went through the door and saw that no one was there. She checked for traces of Damon, but there was nothing.

Ashlie walked out and moved on to the second house which she scanned through the window. The house was empty except for a bag on the floor. She returned to where Silver was standing, and said, "No signs of Damon."

"Yeah, me neither."

Jimmy had gone to the farthest house. Inside there were lots of different weapons stacked up against the back wall. He strolled over and picked up an axe; it was the perfect weight for him. He swung it a couple of times then put it down. There was a crossbow in the corner; he picked it up and took a practice shot.

He replaced it next to the axe, smiled to himself, and walked out of the room.

When he reached the girls, he said, "No Damon."

"Yeah, maybe he escaped," Silver suggested.

Ashlie replied, "I doubt that very much; he was stabbed through the leg. I bet he couldn't even walk after that."

"Where to now?" Silver asked.

"If we're gonna find him, I think we have to get closer to where we saw the villagers earlier," Jimmy replied, walking past the two of them and back to the edge of the wood. Silver and Angalie followed Jimmy.

They stayed hidden amongst the trees, hoping not to be seen. "I see more houses," Jimmy called from the front.

"Wait, stop. There's two men by those houses," Silver called back.

The three of them stopped and looked at the men; Ashlie said, "We must be quite near the villagers now, I guess."

"Yeah, I guess so," Jimmy replied.

"There are only two men," Silver said. "I think we can take them."

Jimmy responded, "No, if they see us, they might alert the others, and I doubt we can take more than two."

"Okay, so what now?" Ashlie asked.

"We could try to sneak in without them seeing us," Jimmy proposed.

"Yeah, good plan, or we could use a decoy, and when they run towards the decoy, the other two go behind and take them out," Silver suggested.

Jimmy asked, "Who's gonna be the decoy?"

Jimmy and Silver both looked at Ashlie.

"Hell, no!" she said.

"C'mon, you won't be in any danger, I promise. Plus, Silver and I have had training," said Jimmy, trying to reassure her.

Ashlie stood staring at them for a few seconds then said, "Okay, for Damon."

"Perfect. We'll give you a signal to step out of the woods, and then we will sneak behind and take them out," Silver said as she and Jimmy drew their swords.

"What's the signal?"

Silver pointed at the tree and said, "I'll throw a stone at that tree, and then you walk out, okay?"

Ashlie nodded and replied, "Um, all right. I'll be ready."

Silver and Jimmy sidled over to the far trees, careful not to be seen by the two men. Ashlie nervously waited for the signal. With their swords ready in their hands, Silver picked up a large stone and hurled it at the top of the tree. When Ashlie heard the stone hit the tree, her heart started thumping, she began to shake, but using all her courage, she walked out into the open so the men could see her. When the two men saw her; they muttered something to each other, drew their swords, and walked slowly towards her. Ashlie shook harder as they approached.

From behind, Jimmy and Silver crept on their tiptoes towards the men. They sped across the open ground without being heard and skewered them both, running their swords through their backs. Both men fell to the ground in front of Ashlie, who shrieked and immediately covered her mouth to stop the sound.

Silver smirked, "Told you I wouldn't let you get hurt."

"Very funny," Ashlie snapped, not amused.

"What should we do with the bodies?" Jimmy asked, looking at the two men.

"Let's drag them to the trees so they won't be found," Silver said as she started dragging one of the bodies.

Jimmy did the same.

Ashlie asked, "What now?"

Silver replied, "Well, we know where the people are, so we need to stay clear of them. We also need to find where they're keeping Damon."

***

Pulling at the chains and the bolt in the wall, Rosalie asked, "Do you think we'll ever get out of here?"

Damon grabbed his chain, spun it in his hand, and replied, "I don't think so."

He stopped when he heard the dungeon door opening. Coralie walked in. They stared at her, waiting for her to speak.

"Your friend didn't make it," Coralie said.

She was upset that King's blood could not help her sister.

"What did you do to him?" Bellomie asked.

Coralie didn't answer.

"So, what now?" Damon asked.

She turned to Damon and responded, "The doctors will try again tomorrow with one of you. Tonight, we will search for more people for blood samples."

"Our families, you mean?" Rosalie asked nervously.

Coralie replied, "Whoever we find; maybe your families, maybe not."

The three of them stared at her in disbelief as she walked out.

"I can't believe King is dead," Bellomie said as he tugged on his chain, trying to pull it from the wall.

They sat back and waited, knowing that one of them would die tomorrow.

***

As Jimmy, Ashlie, and Silver hid in the trees, they heard a commotion coming in their direction.

Ashlie said, "Hear that? It sounds like people."

The three stayed hidden in the trees. Looking out, they saw dozens of people coming towards them, led by a small woman.

"That's a lot of people," Jimmy whispered.

"Yeah, but where are they going?" Silver asked.

"I don't see Damon with them," Ashlie remarked.

"If he's with them, he'll probably be at the back," Silver said. "Let's wait for them to pass and then we'll see. If he's not with them, he may be in the village."

As the villagers passed by, Ashlie remarked, "I still don't see Damon. Where is he?"

Jimmy watched as the last person finally passed them and said, "Let's go check the castle; he may be there."

"Okay, good idea," Ashlie agreed.

Staying in the shadows, the three of them started creeping towards the castle.

They got to the gates of the castle, but when they tried to open them, they found that the gates were locked.

"I don't think he's in the castle," Ashlie said.

"Yeah, I think you might be right," Jimmy replied.

At the same instant, Ashlie and Jimmy both noticed two men guarding an entrance.

"Do you think he's in there?" Silver asked, staring at the guards.

Jimmy replied, "Yeah, I'm pretty sure he is."

"What's the plan this time?" Ashlie asked Jimmy and Silver.

"Care to be the decoy again?" Jimmy asked, laughing.

"No," Ashlie snapped angrily.

"Okay, I guess we'll just fight them without a decoy," Silver said, chuckling. "It should be okay, as the rest of the people have gone."

Jimmy replied, "All right."

Pointing to the entrance, Silver said to Ashlie, "When they come at us, sneak behind them and see what's in there."

Ashlie nodded.

Silver and Jimmy drew their swords and walked towards the guards whilst Ashlie stayed hidden.

The guard to the left of the tunnel drew his sword and attacked Silver. Swinging frantically left and right, Silver stepped back, blocking his attacks. She swung with her left elbow and knocked him onto his back. She stepped forward and stabbed him through the stomach, quickly pulling the sword back out.

Jimmy walked towards the guard on the right, who held an axe. He was big but slow, and when he swung his axe, Jimmy just stepped to the side, avoiding contact. He did it again, and on the third swing, Jimmy stepped forward and slit the guard's throat.

Whilst on their training course, Roan had showed them how to use fighting techniques to survive a kill-or-be-killed situation. As they fought, Ashlie made her way through the entrance and down a tunnel and came to a big wooden door to the dungeons. She tried to open it, but it was locked, so she sprinted back to Silver and Jimmy.

Ashlie saw the two dead guards on the ground and said, "Well, that must have been easy."

"Yeah, I guess it was," Silver replied.

"I found a door down there," Ashlie said, "but it's locked. "Damon may be inside."

Silver suggested, "Let's check the guards; see if they have any keys on them."

They searched the guards' pockets but found nothing.

"If you had an important key, where would you keep it?" Ashlie asked.

Silver replied, "Probably around my neck, if it wasn't in my pocket."

Silver checked one of the guards. He was wearing a necklace of bones, and in the centre, was a bronze key tied by a string. She ripped the key off and asked, "Could this be it?"

"Yeah, maybe," Ashlie replied. "Let's see."

Silver stood up holding the key, and they all headed to the tunnel.

At the dungeon door, Silver handed the key to Ashlie, and she pushed it into the lock.

***

On the other side of the door, the prisoners heard scratching.

Damon got to his feet quickly, scared at the outcome, but then asked, "Who could that be?"

"Don't know," Bellomie replied, also getting to his feet.

Ashlie had forced open the door and poked her head inside.

"Ashlie!" Damon shouted as he saw her.

Ashlie ran over to him, and gave him a massive hug.

Jimmy and Silver followed after her. They saw Rosalie and Bellomie standing in the corner.

Silver cried, "Rosalie!"

She walked over and hugged her.

Jimmy walked over to Bellomie, grabbed his forearm, patted him on the back, and said, "I knew we'd meet again."

"How did you find us?" Bellomie asked. "Where are Angalie, Josh, and Jenavieve?"

"They're safe," Jimmy said confidently. "They went back to Ville de Parie."

Looking upset, Damon said, "What? There is nothing there. That's why we left. It's been destroyed."

"Where's Julien?" Jimmy asked.

"After they captured us," Rosalie said, sobbing, "they killed him to make us cooperate."

"Oh, we're so sorry," Silver replied sympathetically.

"King also got captured," Rosalie said. "He's dead too."

Silver asked, "What happened?"

"They needed his blood, but something went wrong."

Bellomie said, "Tomorrow, they're coming for our blood."

"So, let's get out of here," Damon said. "Do you have the key for these chains?"

"Yeah, here," Ashlie said.

After they were unchained, they hurried out of the dungeons.

"I heard them talking about finding our families and taking their blood to test for the cure," Damon said as he walked out of the tunnel. "We must find our families before Coralie does."

They all nodded in agreement, and Jimmy said, "Yeah, good idea. Let's go."

Chapter 10

Slowly Rebuilding

*J*enavieve, Angalie, and Josh were staring blankly at their destroyed home, Ville de Parie, when they heard something in the distance.

Startled, Angalie asked, "What was that?"

"I don't know," Jenavieve replied. "It came from over there." She walked towards her house to see what had made the noise.

Pointing to the damaged house, Josh shouted, "There, I think I see someone."

The three of them strode over, and in the house, they saw a young man moving planks of broken wood out of the way. He was wearing a dirty white shirt, dark blue shorts, and a hat. He moved like a rat scavenging for food.

Jenavieve clambered over to him and asked, "Hey, what are you doing?"

The man shook his head, moving his long hair out of his face. He turned to Jenavieve and replied, "I'm looking for food. I'm starving; leave me alone."

"This was my house; I used to live here," Jenavieve said. "Where did everyone go?"

The man stared at Jenavieve and asked, "Where's the food?"

Josh and Angalie shuffled forward and stood next to Jenavieve, and Angalie said, "We'll show you if you tell us where everyone went."

"Hmm, fine," the man replied. "My village was destroyed by the meteors. Everyone who survived was slaughtered. Luckily, I was taking a swim at a nearby waterfall when I heard the screams from my village. I didn't want to be next, so I ran away. I came here and saw that everyone was running that way; they were all heading north."

Josh looked north to where he had pointed and sighed, "We've just come from there."

"Now, where's the food?" the man asked, as saliva dripped from his mouth.

Jenavieve showed him where the kitchen used to be and said, "All right, a deal is a deal. If there was any food, it would be here. I doubt there's any left now, though."

The man quickly scrambled past her; they moved some rubble from the floor and found some cartons of food.

"Wait, you said your village was slaughtered?" Angalie asked. "Who by?"

"We call them the mutated men. They kill everyone and feast on them. We tried to fight them, but everyone was killed."

"Oh, that's awful," Angalie said.

Still looking for more food, the young man muttered, "It doesn't matter; it's over now. I found a way to avoid them. I knew I had to get out and leave before they found me."

Josh asked, "What's your name? And where is this waterfall?" Smelling his armpits, he continued, "I could do with a wash."

"I'm Theo. I can show you the waterfall," he said. "It's not far."

Theo found some more food and exclaimed, "Finally!" He quickly scoffed down the food. "It's this way to the waterfall."

The four of them climbed over the rubble and followed a trail towards the mountain. There were craters in the ground where the meteors had hit, and they had to be careful to avoid falling in. When they arrived at the mountain, they saw a white waterfall falling into a large deep pool. The water was clear; sharp rocks surrounded the pool, and they could see smooth circular rocks at the bottom. Josh quickly took off his shirt and shorts; he jumped in, submerging and then coming back up.

He put his hands through his hair and said, "Oh, my God; it's so refreshing. You have to come in."

The other three stared at him and then slipped out of their clothes and jumped in too, leaving their spears at the side of the pool.

"It's so nice," Angalie said as she swam towards the waterfall and let it cascade onto her back. "Jenavieve, come, it's like a spa."

The other three swam over to the waterfall and sat under it, letting the water hit them too. They stayed at the waterfall for ages. Once they felt clean enough, the four of them got out and put on their clothes.

As they picked up their spears, Jenavieve said, "We need to find our parents."

Angalie asked, "Do you think they're okay?"

"Yeah," Josh and Jenavieve nodded in agreement.

"I can take you north, if that's the way you want to go," Theo said. "I know a safe route; it used to be impassable, but now the meteors have cleared the way. We can head there easily, if you want."

"Okay, great," Angalie said, smiling.

They all started walking back down the mountain. Theo led the way and said, "It's still a hard walk, but it should be okay."

Looking at the long road ahead, the three of them thought about their parents and wondered if they were okay or not.

***

Their parents were heading north too, going slowly through the snow. They were tired, and their feet were swollen. They had walked for days. They could see the damaged airport where their children's plane had arrived earlier.

Jenavieve's mother, Sarabella, asked everyone, "What happened here?"

Looking around at the demolished surroundings, Lilly, Josh's mum, replied, "I don't know. Looks like the same thing that happened to our homes."

They heard a man shouting in the distance, "Lift, lift, easy does it."

"Looks like someone is giving orders," Angalie's father Leo said. His wife, Isabelle, nodded.

Billie was attempting to get the people who had arrived to try and rebuild the village by the airport. The four of them carried on. They stopped to watch workers as they lifted a large gate into place.

"Wow, looks like they've done a lot of work," Lilly commented, looking around.

When Billie spotted them, he immediately went to greet them, "Hi, welcome. Have you come a long way? We are slowly rebuilding our village. Like everything else, this place was destroyed by the meteors."

"I can see. Good job," Sarabella replied, nodding in appreciation.

Leo turned to Billie and asked, "So are you in charge?"

"Yeah, I guess so. No one else wanted to take charge, so I did. Which town have you guys come from?"

"We are from Ville de Parie," Sarabella said. "I'm looking for my children, Jenavieve and Ashlie. I had hoped that they would be here."

Lilly added, "And I hoped to find my son, Josh."

"And we hoped to find our daughter, Angalie," Leo and Isabelle interjected.

"Oh, I'm sorry," Billie said. "They were here, but they left, along with some other people. They went to find you."

"How about Ashlie?" Sarabella asked. "She was with an older boy, Damon. Were they here?"

Billie shook his head, "Sorry, no, they haven't turned up yet."

"If there is anything we can do to help, please let us know," Leo said.

"Yeah, we need to keep our minds busy," Isabelle added.

"Okay," Billie said. "There's a lot of stuff we need help with. We need to erect those tents, and if you're up for a challenge, some houses need to be built. Ask around; the people here will help you if you ask. The big man over there is Roan; he's in charge of tents and house-building."

They walked over to Roan. Sarabella asked, "How can we help?"

He nodded his head towards some tents and replied, "You see those tents over there? They all need to be put up."

People had started putting tents up already, but there were many more to go. The people from the outlying towns had come together and were working on rebuilding the village.

Surveying the mountains, Lilly said, "With all the tall buildings gone, you can really see the nice scenery."

A fast-moving stream ran down the mountain, flowing into a large lake. The sun shone on them as they started helping with the tents. There was a cool breeze too, which was nice. As they worked, they started sweating. It took them ages to get the tents up, but it kept their minds off their children.

Roan called out, "Good job, everyone. Take some rest, and we'll start again in an hour."

Billie had built a lookout tower in the centre of the village.

He climbed to the top and shouted, "I need some volunteers who will help me build some defences on the wall. We don't know what is out there, but we need to keep safe in case something bad does come."

Four men stepped forward and began discussing how they would protect their new home.

Billie said, "Before we do anything, we need weapons."

"What? How are we gonna get weapons?" one of the men asked.

"I have an idea," another man said. "We can make arrows using wood from the trees. We can also dig a moat and fill it with water from the lake."

"Yes, all good ideas," Billie said, "but first, we need to find steel to make swords."

He turned and headed back toward his tent.

The men watched him walk away; one of them said, "He always goes back to his tent. I wonder what's so important in there."

"Maybe he's got a woman in there," the second man joked.

"I doubt it," the other retorted.

After Billie went back into his tent, he sat down, opened his bag, and lifted something out of it. It was his voice-activated, state-of-the-art computer.

He asked the computer, "Where can I find steel near my location, and what's a good way to construct a defensive wall?"

The computer showed a map of his location and the surrounding towns, and also where he could find steel. It then showed the best defence system for a wall.

Billie walked back to the four men and said, "The moat around the wall is a good idea; get started on that. We also need some large rocks or boulders we can place on the top of the wall."

Pointing at three of the men, he continued, "You three go find the rocks and boulders."

He turned to the other volunteer and said, "You and I will go to find the steel. Hey, what's your name, by the way?"

"Oliver" came the reply, "but you can call me Ollie"

Billie and Ollie headed out in search of the steel. Billie had copied the map from the computer onto a piece of paper. They moved through the forest, walking fast.

Billie said, "We have to find the steel and get back before sundown. I don't want to be out here when it's dark."

"Yeah, me neither," Ollie replied.

Just then, Billie came to a halt. He turned to Ollie, smiled, and said, "It's here."

Ollie looked around and scoffed, "There's nothing here."

"It must be underground," Billie said.

They looked for ages, feeling the ground, and then Ollie shouted to Billie, "Over here. I think I found something."

Billie walked over to him and saw a round object that looked like a manhole cover.

He ran his hands along the cover and asked, "What are those markings?"

"I don't know," Ollie replied, staring intently at the markings.

Billie took out the piece of paper and started drawing the markings.

"Try to find a lever so we can open the cover and see if there's any steel down there."

Ollie dug away some more soil and said, "What's this?"

He was holding a long, steel crowbar.

Billie finished the drawing, put it in his pocket, and walked over to Ollie. They levered the manhole cover and opened it together. As they moved the cover away, the shaft below emitted a cool waft of stale, musty air.

Peering into the hole, Ollie asked, "What's that down there?"

"I don't know. Let's go check it out."

Chapter 11

Poisonous Waters

Silver and the others walked back towards the village.

"There are some weapons in that house," Jimmy said. "We should get some to protect ourselves."

When they reached the house, Jimmy opened the door and said, "There are a lot of weapons here. I'm gonna keep my sword and get another, and that crossbow. You should all get some too."

Jimmy put the two swords across his back in an x-shape and then picked up the crossbow. He aimed it at the door and pretended to shoot it.

Staring at the weapons, Damon said, "I don't really know how to fight, so I would be useless with any of these."

An Unfinished Event

"Yeah, same here," Ashlie added, lowering her head.

"That's okay," Silver said, grabbing Ashlie's shoulder and pushing her towards the weapons. "We can train you."

Silver already had a sword across her back. She picked up two Chinese throwing stars and put them in her pockets. She then held out two smaller swords to Ashlie.

"Take these," Silver said. "These should keep you safe, once I train you."

Ashlie replied, "Thanks."

"Put them on your back, like this," Silver said, crossing the swords on her back and placing them in her belt.

Bellomie picked up a sword and tested the weight. "Try this," he said, handing it to Damon. "How does it feel?"

Damon took the sword, held it with both hands, and then started swinging.

He turned to Bellomie and said," It's good; it's the perfect weight."

"Good, that can be your weapon," Bellomie said as he picked up a sword for himself and slipped it into his waist belt.

He knelt down, picked up two knives, and put those into his belt too.

"I'm ready."

Rosalie grabbed two swords and said, "Me too."

"Okay, let's go," Jimmy said, leading the way out of the room.

Silver called to him, "They have food in the other house; we should stock up for the journey north."

"Yeah, good idea," Jimmy replied, walking over to the house where they had seen the food.

"I think I saw a bag in one of the houses," Ashlie said. "I'll go check." She walked alone back to the house.

There was no one around. The silence scared her. She looked back towards the others, but they were already inside the other house. As she walked up to the door; she thought that she heard something behind her. She quickly turned to see what it was, but nothing was there; it could have been the wind in the trees.

The door was locked. Ashlie walked round to a window and peered in. She could see the bag on the floor. Frustrated, she took out one of her swords and shattered the glass in the window. It was a tight fit, but she squeezed her way through and flopped on to the floor, avoiding the broken glass. She picked up the bag and walked to the window, chucked the bag through the window, climbed out and walked back to the others. They had already gathered most of the food.

"Got the bag," Ashlie said, throwing it on the floor.

"You took your time," Silver said, putting a slab of meat inside the bag.

"The door was locked," she snapped. "I had to break the window to get in."

"Are you okay?" Damon asked, putting another piece of meat in the bag.

"Yeah, I'm fine." She checked the weight of the bag and asked, "Maybe we can take turns carrying the bag; it's pretty heavy."

"Yeah, that way it's fair," Bellomie said, picking up the bag and slinging it over his shoulder. "I'll take the first shift."

The six of them walked to the edge of the village. There were mountains in the distance and forests to the left and right of them.

Jimmy looked at the sun, worked out which way was north, and with the sun on his back, said, "They would have gone this way; let's go."

Ashlie informed the others, "That's where the mutated men are."

"Yes, but we have weapons now to protect us," Jimmy replied, as he peered at the mountains in the distance.

Silver patted Ashlie on the back, reassuring her, and said, "Don't worry. We'll protect you if they come."

"Okay, let's go then," she replied, trying not to think about the mutated men.

They all followed Silver. As they walked through the forest, they could feel the cool air on their faces and hear many varieties of insects, buzzing and chirping and squeaking.

As they hiked towards the mountain, Bellomie asked, "How far do you think it is?"

Jimmy said, "No idea; there is no scale on the map. It may take a couple of days; depends on what we come across."

From the front, Silver heard Damon say, "What's the plan if we encounter something?"

She answered, "Try to stay hidden. It would be stupid to engage anything dangerous. But if we have to . . ."

She strode on, continuing up the mountain. Damon thought about what she said as he followed after her.

The mountain slope started to level off. They walked more slowly to catch their breath.

Ashlie called from the back, "Can we take a break for a sec?"

"Yeah, this bag of meat is heavy," Bellomie said, dropping the bag on the ground.

Jimmy picked up the bag, and said, "I'll take it for now; you've been carrying it long enough. We'll take a short break, but then we have to push on."

Silver sat down next to Rosalie and said, "You okay? A short break, plus we need to find some water soon."

After their rest, Rosalie got to her feet and said, "I guess there's a stream in these mountains, maybe even a waterfall."

The ground was rough as they carried on and after hiking around a bend, the path was blocked by some large boulders.

Rosalie reached them first and said, "Hmm, any ideas?"

The rest caught up with her and looked to see if there was a way around the boulders.

Jimmy put down the bag of meat and said, "We need to get over them somehow."

They all stared at the boulders.

Bellomie said to Jimmy, "If you get on my shoulders, I think you can reach the top."

Jimmy looked at Bellomie and then at the boulder, "It's worth a try."

"You sure?" Ashlie asked, worrying about Jimmy's safety.

Jimmy looked at the boulders again and said, "Yeah, let's do this."

Bellomie knelt in front of the boulder with his hands in the air. Jimmy grabbed Bellomie's hands and put his feet on his shoulders. Bellomie stood up, straining under the weight. Rosalie and Silver stood next to Bellomie, holding his arms to keep him balanced. Jimmy let go of Bellomie's hands and reached up, also trying to keep his balance.

"I'm gonna jump and try to grab the top; catch me if I fall."

Bellomie braced himself and replied, "Okay."

Jimmy bent his legs and leapt off Bellomie's shoulders, pushing off the boulder with one foot and grabbing the top with his fingers. He threw his other arm up, getting a better grip. He pulled himself up the boulder, swung his feet round and flopped forward at the top.

He shouted down to the others, "I'm up; throw me the bag."

Bellomie hurled the bag up and asked, "What can you see?"

Jimmy turned and looked around. He could see a stream which led to a lake and beyond that, a crater in the mountain. The sun was shining bright, and he could see the whole landscape from the boulder.

He turned back to Bellomie and said, "Amazing view from up here. Now you need to do the same with everyone else; put them on your shoulders, and I'll pull them up. Damon first."

One by one, they all got on Bellomie's shoulders, and Jimmy pulled them up. After helping Ashlie up, Bellomie looked up at Jimmy and asked, "What about me?"

Jimmy turned to Damon and said, "You and Ashlie, hold my legs tight. I'll reach down to him. When I'm holding him, all of you pull me up, okay?"

They nodded in agreement. Jimmy lowered himself down the boulder, with Damon and Ashlie holding his legs, whilst Rosalie and Silver waited to help pull him up.

Jimmy called to Bellomie and said, "Run, jump off those rocks, and reach for my hands. We'll pull you up."

"Okay," Bellomie said, taking a few steps back before running towards the boulder.

He ran, jumped, but missed Jimmy's hands.

"C'mon, again," Jimmy said, gesturing to him.

Bellomie shook his head, took three strides back, and then ran at the boulder again. He sprang off the rocks, reached for Jimmy's hands again, but missed. Jimmy instinctively grabbed his forearms.

He yelled to Rosalie and Silver, "Pull me up!" He gripped Bellomie's arms tightly but didn't know how long he could hold him for.

Bellomie used his feet to push himself up the boulder whilst Jimmy held on to him. With a final burst of energy, they pulled him to the top. Jimmy fell back into Damon and Ashlie, with Bellomie on top of him.

Bellomie looked up and saw the lake and asked, "Wow, that looks nice; do you think it's clean?"

"Clean enough," Jimmy replied as Bellomie helped him up.

Bellomie grinned and said, "Thanks for not leaving me."

Jimmy patted his shoulder and replied, "No problem."

Jimmy looked down; there were two smaller boulders in between them and the lake. He picked up the bag and crossbow and jumped down past the boulders towards the lake. The others followed.

When they reached the lake, Silver took off her clothes and jumped in. She was so thirsty she had to drink the water even though she knew she probably shouldn't.

The others watched her to make sure that it was safe.

Silver lifted her head out of the water and said, "Seems safe."

"Drink as much as you want to, and then we need to carry on," Jimmy said as he took a huge gulp of water.

They finished drinking, put their clothes back on, and then headed out again, still keeping their bearing north. They came to the edge of the crater and started to walk round it.

Halfway round, Ashlie said, "I don't feel so good."

"Yeah, me neither," Damon said, holding his stomach.

Rosalie bent over double and vomited onto the ground; after wiping her chin, she said, "Yeah, I think that water might have been bad."

Bellomie walked back and held his sister until she finished vomiting.

He took a deep breath and exhaled slowly, saying, "I feel fine; how about you two?"

Jimmy and Silver took deep breaths, and Jimmy said, "I'm okay; whatever was in the water didn't affect me."

Silver took another deep breath, "I'm good too."

Jimmy walked over to Ashlie and Damon; he asked, "Are you okay to carry on walking?"

They both gave him a thumbs up.

Bellomie looked down at Rosalie and asked, "Can you walk?"

Rosalie coughed and then replied, "Yeah, I think I got most of it out."

The six of them carried on walking; they passed the crater and started to climb another mountain.

"There's a path leading down the mountain. I think we should take it," Jimmy remarked.

Bellomie held his sister, and Jimmy supported Ashlie and Damon with both arms as they walked on. Silver was carrying the bag of food now. They got to the bottom of the mountain and were in a valley with mountains rising on either side of them. Trees and bushes were all around them.

Silver suddenly stopped and called out, "Wait, I think I see something. Stay here."

Jimmy helped Ashlie and Damon lay down and walked over to Silver.

He gave her his crossbow and said, "Take this."

She ran off up the mountain with the crossbow. The other five sat down and waited.

Ashlie still felt sick; she asked softly, "What do you think she saw?"

"No idea, but she'll be back soon," Jimmy predicted, watching Silver disappear out of sight.

Bellomie asked, "How are you three feeling?"

Damon and Ashlie looked at each other; their faces were swollen.

Damon replied, "I'm still feeling a bit sick."

Rosalie said, "I'm feeling a lot better now after throwing up. Maybe that's what you need to do to feel better."

"How do you suppose we do that?" Ashlie asked.

Rosalie said, "I don't know, maybe stick your fingers down your throat and force it out."

"Eww, no way," Ashlie replied, revolted at the thought. "That's disgusting."

Bellomie looked at Damon, "It might be the only way."

Damon felt faint and knew whatever he'd drunk was making him feel sick. But the thought of sticking his fingers down his throat made him feel worse.

He turned to Jimmy and said, "I can't do it. Can you do it for me?"

Jimmy looked at him for a moment and then said, "What? Are you serious? You want me to stick my fingers down your throat?"

"Yes, please," Damon said, looking at him for comfort.

They all looked at Jimmy and Damon anxiously.

Jimmy looked back at them and said, "Okay, I'll do it, but someone else has to do it for Ashlie."

"Done," Damon said eagerly.

"What? No, I don't agree to this," Ashlie snapped.

Jimmy ignored her and walked up to Damon.

He said to Bellomie, "Hold his head and keep his mouth open. Don't let him bite my fingers."

Bellomie grabbed Damon's head, and forced his mouth open. Jimmy closed his eyes and stuck two fingers deep down Damon's throat, held them there for a second, and then pulled them out. Bellomie let go of Damon, who jumped forward and vomited all over the ground. Water and blood projected out of his mouth. Then he vomited again, but this time, he spat out a hairy black bug with claws; it fell onto the ground and began eating the blood. Jimmy went over to it and stamped on it.

He looked down at the mangled creature and said, "What the hell is that?"

Ashlie looked at the creature and said, "Is that what's inside me?"

"Yeah, and it's feeding off your blood," Bellomie said. "We have to get it out, or it will feed off all your blood."

Ashlie looked drained and finally said, "Okay."

Bellomie grabbed her head, pulled it back, and opened her mouth; he said, "Rosalie, stick your fingers down her throat."

Rosalie walked over and stuck her fingers down Ashlie's throat. As she pulled them out, something bit her fingers. She screamed in pain and pulled her hand out of Ashlie's mouth; another big bug was still attached to her fingers.

"Holy moly, that's huge," Damon said, looking at the creature.

Ashlie instantly threw up all over Jimmy and Rosalie's hands, and then she fell to the ground, unconscious. Bellomie held her as she lay on the ground.

The creature was still biting Rosalie's fingers, sucking her blood. Jimmy walked over and grabbed the bug, threw it on the ground, and then stamped on it, killing it.

Rosalie shook her hand and said, "Damn, that hurt, no wonder she passed out."

"Get her some water," Jimmy ordered Damon.

Damon got some water and then brought it back to Jimmy.

Ashlie still lay unconscious as Rosalie asked, "Is she alive? She looks dead."

Bellomie checked her pulse and said, "Barely, we need to wake her up and give her some water."

Jimmy looked at her and slapped her face gently to wake her up. The other three took a step back to give Ashlie some breathing space, waiting for her to come to. Ashlie made a little noise. Jimmy held her head and said, "Drink, you need to gain your strength. That creature was sucking your blood."

Ashlie sat up slowly and took a sip of water.

Damon sat next to her and asked, "How are you feeling?"

"A bit better," she replied quietly. "Thanks."

Rosalie looked up at the mountainside where Silver had gone and asked, "Where is Silver? She's been gone for ages."

"Yeah, it's been a while," Jimmy replied.

Up the mountain, Silver was pursuing the man she had seen. Keeping an eye on him, she sped up to a jog, her crossbow pointed at him. The man stopped when he came to a meadow strewn with meteorites. Silver waited in the trees watching him jump from one to another. She aimed the crossbow and shot, but missed. The man smirked; looking right at her after the arrow clattered harmlessly against a large meteorite. He was wearing a skull mask; he turned and started running away. Silver restrung her crossbow and ran into the meadow and took aim, but he was no longer in sight. She climbed onto one of the rocks so she could see where he was running to.

The man dodged in and out of the meteorites to avoid getting hit by her arrows. He thought he was out of range, so he stopped, took out a large horn and was about to blow it, when one of Silver's arrows struck him in the back of the head. The man fell to the ground, dropping the horn.

Silver slowly walked up to him, picked up the horn, and recognised his mask. He was a scout from Coralie's village. From the top of the mountain, she looked down and saw people walking in the distance. She sighed to herself and muttered, "Coralie's villagers."

Chapter 12

Searching for a Cure

*C*oralie and the people from her village were marching through the forest. She had sent out a scout to make sure that they were heading in the right direction. The scout still hadn't returned. Coralie was getting desperate; she couldn't wait any longer. She needed to find the cure to save her sister who had been mutated by the virus.

The villagers emerged from the forest and found themselves in a valley surrounded by high mountains. Coralie was leading. Her two advisers were walking beside her.

She asked one of the advisers, *"Where's the scout? I sent him out ages ago; he should be back by now."*

The adviser suggested, *"He might have gotten lost or had some difficulty."*

An Unfinished Event

They stopped at a large river in the valley; Coralie ordered another scout be sent to find the first one.

She knelt at the riverbank and dipped her hand into the water to check the strength of the current.

"The current's not that strong. We can cross here."

One advisor shouted to the other villagers, *"Ew era gion ot sor ti."*

The people looked at Coralie and the advisors, and then they nodded twice in acknowledgement, as was their custom.

Coralie waded into the river to cross it. There were sharp stones on the riverbed, causing her to stumble. As she got farther into the river, the stones were smaller and smoother. These stones were slippery but she kept her balance. The water was clear, with white foam on the surface. She got to the other bank and looked back at her people, who were slowly making their way down to the river. Once they had all crossed, they carried on marching through the muddy ground. Coralie could see a clearing in the distance.

She pointed ahead and told her advisors, *"I think that clearing is large enough to hold all of us. Let's make camp there."*

The advisors nodded their agreement. Coralie led the villagers into the large open space. The people stopped behind her.

She shouted in her mother tongue, "*We can stay here tonight.*"

The villagers began erecting the tents that they had brought with them. Coralie and her two advisors also put up their tent.

By the time all the tents were up, it had grown dark. Coralie sat on the ground with her two advisers either side of her in the biggest tent in the centre of the camp.

She stood up and said, "*We need a big fire in the middle of the camp to keep everyone warm and ward off the mutants.*"

"*Yes, Coralie,*" the two replied as they stood up. They left the tent immediately to organise the lighting of the fire.

The second scout that Coralie had sent out had returned. He was taken to Coralie's tent.

When she saw the man, she asked, "*What did you find?*"

The scout held up the arrow that had killed the previous scout.

He approached Coralie and said, "*I found the scout; he's dead. This was in the back of his head, and his horn was missing.*"

He handed the bloody arrow to Coralie, who asked, "*Did you see who did this?*"

"*No, there was no one around, but that arrow is one of ours.*"

Coralie, shocked, snapped, "*What do you mean, one of ours?*"

"*Look at the markings on the arrow,*" the scout replied, pointing.

Coralie wiped off the blood with a cloth and looked closely at the arrow. "*You're right; it is.*"

She grew angry but kept her cool as she issued her orders.

"*Head back to the castle and check the dungeons. See if the prisoners have escaped, and report back to me.*"

"*Yes, Coralie,*" the scout replied, saluting before turning and heading out of the tent.

The campfire was lit, and some of the villagers stood around it, warming their hands. Coralie left her tent and walked towards the fire. As she reached it, the villagers all turned to her. When she spoke, she spoke loudly enough for everyone to hear.

"Get some food and rest; ready for the hike. I have a feeling we will find people tomorrow to get blood samples from."

Then she turned and walked back to her tent.

Meanwhile, the second scout hurried back over the river, through the forest, and on to the castle to check on the prisoners. He entered the village and marched toward the houses. Looking into the first house, he saw that the food had been taken. He raced over to the weapons house and saw that they were gone too. He thought to himself that the prisoners must have escaped. He went to the castle and crept cautiously towards the tunnel leading to the dungeons. Seeing two dead men laying outside the tunnel, he instantly realised that the prisoners must have escaped. He drew his sword and warily entered the tunnel. He saw that the door to the dungeon was open, so he ran towards it. Putting a hand on the door, he looked inside and saw the chains on the ground and no prisoners.

He muttered to himself, *"Coralie was right."*

The scout came back out of the tunnel and saw that the horses were still in the stables. He was tired but knew he had to get back to Coralie. He took her horse and rode back through the forest, over the fields, and across the river. It was late but that didn't stop him. He rode in to the centre of camp, jumped off the horse, and went to her tent. Coralie was asleep on a blanket on the ground. He walked over and shook her shoulder to wake her. She turned, grabbed his arm, and held an arrow to his throat.

Looking down at her, he said, *"Please don't kill the messenger."*

Coralie dropped the arrow and asked, *"What did you find out?"*

The scout replied, *"It's what you thought; they escaped. I found three dead guards, two outside the dungeon and one other in the trees. The prisoners must have had help escaping."*

Coralie sat up, grabbed the scout's shoulder, and snapped, *"Yes, it seems that way, doesn't it? Find them. In the morning, we will head north; catch up with us after you capture them."*

"Yes, Coralie," the scout replied, saluting as he walked out of the tent. He got ready to travel through the night again in search of the prisoners.

Next morning Coralie was up before anyone else. The sun shone brightly; Coralie strode out of her tent, shielding her eyes. Her two advisors stood motionless beside her. She walked to the middle of the camp where she could best be seen and blew her horn, waking everyone.

Once the villagers emerged from their tents, she yelled, "*Let's go!*"

Chapter 13

Steel Weapons

Billie and Ollie started climbing down the ladder in the long, dark shaft. They had gone in search of steel to forge weapons so that after they received some training, they could defend themselves.

The shaft was cold as ice.

From above, Ollie asked, "What do you think is down there?"

Billie looked down and said, "No idea, but this ladder goes down pretty far."

Ollie held on tight and gulped as he looked down past Billie. Suddenly, the manhole cover at the surface slammed shut with a loud boom; they were in complete darkness. Trapped.

Billie looked up and said, "What was that?"

Ollie replied, "I think that the manhole cover shut."

"We have to keep going. I have a lighter in my pocket; we'll be able to see when we get to the bottom," Billie declared.

As they continued to climb down the shaft, Billie could sense he was nearly at the bottom. He tested with his foot to see if there was one more rung on the ladder, but there wasn't. He dropped to the ground and landed on what he thought was mud. He lit his lighter to see. Looking down, he saw it was a mangled body covered in spiderwebs. The stench was overpowering.

When Ollie finally got to the bottom, Billie said, "I don't think we're alone down here."

Billie shone the lighter on the body so that Ollie could see. He jumped back in shock and squeezed his nostrils shut. Next to the body, Billie saw a sword, covered in more spiderwebs. He grabbed the hilt, but the web was so tight around the sword that he couldn't move it.

Ollie was still holding his nose and muttering to himself.

Billie said, "Hey, help me get this out. The spider that made this must have been infected or something. No spiderweb is this strong."

Ollie knelt down and tried to rip out the sword, which looked pretty old.

"What is this? Why is this web so strong?" Ollie asked, pulling with all his strength but unable to free the sword from the web.

Billie helped Ollie up and said, "Let me try to burn it out; that might work."

Ollie took a step back and watched as Billie knelt on top of the body and flicked his lighter next to the web. The web sparked and caught fire and burnt away to nothing.

Billie bent over, picked up the sword, and said, "I guess the spider that made this web isn't used to fire."

"Yeah, I guess not."

Billie stood up and said, "I think we are gonna need more fire."

Ollie nodded. "Yeah."

He knelt down next to the body and said, "With his arm and guts, we might be able to make a torch."

Ollie ripped the arm off the decayed body, covered the end with the entrails, and handed it to Billie, saying, "Try to light this up."

Billie grabbed the arm and lit the end, but nothing happened. Meanwhile, Ollie had also made a torch using rags from the dead body. Billie took that torch and set it ablaze. He waved it around to see what was down the dark tunnel.

"Let's go," Billie said as he ventured deeper into the tunnel.

He spotted the same markings on the wall as he had seen earlier on the manhole cover. As they walked through the tunnel, they noticed that the ground was covered in body parts; bones were scattered all around.

Billie shone the torch over the body parts to get a better look; he said, "A lot of people have died down here."

Ollie looked down, saw the bones, but said nothing. He feared that they could be next. As they went farther into the tunnel, the air got colder, and there were spiderwebs all over the ground and walls. Suddenly, a deafening noise echoed through the tunnel; then, dead silence.

Ollie whispered, "What was that?"

Billie felt nervous but kept a brave face and replied, "No idea; let's keep going."

Shaking with fright, they walked through the webs. Billie kept moving the torch from side to side to see what had made the commotion, but it was completely dark ahead.

The webs grew even bigger. This made them more alarmed because they were now realising how big the creature might be. They started walking more slowly. There was the smell of sulphur that came from what they hoped was the end of the tunnel. Billie stopped as he kicked something in the dark. He shone the torch down and saw five dead carcasses lined up in a row, covered in cobwebs. They're rotting flesh smelled as if they had been killed a while ago.

Billie set fire to the spiderweb wrapped around the first body. The flames spread to the next four webs. There was plenty of light now, but the smoke from the burning carcasses made their eyes water. They could make out something moving in the distance.

Ollie noticed a large canvas bag and wondered, "Could that be the bag of steel?"

Billie looked at the movement in the distance and then over to the bag; he replied, "Yeah, I think so."

"I hope you have a plan for whatever's down there," said Ollie.

Keeping his eyes on the dark movement in the distance, Billie replied, "Yes, I have a plan, but it's not a good one."

Ollie asked, "Well, what is it?"

"We scare the creature with fire, then grab the bag, and make a run for it," Billie said.

Ollie looked at Billie, "That's the worst plan I've ever heard. First, the creature might not be afraid of fire, and second, the opening at the top of the ladder is closed, so we can't get out that way."

Billie thought a moment, "Oh, yeah. I forgot. Have you got any ideas?"

Just then, the creature appeared out of the darkness.

Ollie dropped his head to his chest and said, "I think we're gonna have to fight that thing and then find a way out of here."

Billie stared at the creature. He handed his sword to Ollie, and they slowly walked towards the creature.

Billie said, "Use this sword if you have to."

As they approached the creature, the stench got even stronger. There were more bodies covered in webs and they kept getting their feet stuck in them. They were now close to the creature and the canvas bag.

Billie whispered, "Distract the creature, I'll grab the bag."

Ollie inched past Billie to get a better look at the creature and said, "Okay."

Holding the sword tight with both hands, terrified, he crept towards the creature. The creature lifted itself from the ground on eight long, hairy legs. Its body was shaped like a tarantula, but it had a scorpion's tail. Its large head had two sharp fangs; saliva dripped off each of them.

Ollie stepped back, petrified. He froze, unable to move. Billie ran forward and hurled the torch at the creature, trying to scare it. Startled, the creature shook its head as the torch hit it in the face.

Billie sprinted past Ollie and grabbed the bag of steel, shouting, "C'mon."

Still in shock, Ollie could only stand and stare at the creature. Billie ran past him and kept running back through the tunnel towards the shaft to escape, leaving him behind. The creature stomped up to Ollie. Towering above him, it leered down at him, hissing, saliva dripped from its fangs onto Ollie's face. Then it whipped its scorpion-like tail around and pierced Ollie's heart.

He immediately collapsed onto his knees, dropped the sword, and fell to the ground. When Billie looked back, the creature was spinning a web to cocoon Ollie's body.

Still holding the bag, Billie ran as fast as he could to the ladder. As he sprinted through the tunnel, the burning bodies shone enough light for him to see. Finally, he could make out the ladder in the darkness ahead. He could hear the creature's tip-tapping footsteps and hissing behind him; it was very close now. The steel he was carrying was heavy and slowed him down, but he knew he had to get to the ladder, or he was dead too.

When he reached the ladder, his adrenaline kicked in. He started climbing as fast as he could. The creature reached the ladder and whipped its tail up at Billie's leg, but missed him. The creature let out a roar, and the whole tunnel vibrated. Billie held on tightly, praying not to lose his grip. He took a deep breath, relaxed, and kept climbing. He got to the top of the ladder, but when he tried to push the manhole cover, it opened a little but then it dropped shut; it was too heavy to push open all the way.

Billie secured his feet and used all his strength to push the cover open slightly. He squeezed his hands outside so it wouldn't close. He pulled himself up out of the tunnel, and the cover dropped shut behind him. He was still holding the bag tightly.

Billie wasn't sure how long he had been in the tunnel. He could see the village in the distance as he walked back. While he had been away, the villagers had dug a moat and built a drawbridge over it.

From the top of the village wall, a man yelled, "Lower the bridge,"

Billie crossed the bridge, went up to the man, and said, "Good work; you've got a lot done in my absence."

"Thanks." replied the man.

Billie dropped the bag in the centre of the village and shouted, "I got the steel."

Everyone continued working, so Billie went to see Roan and the others, who were erecting tents.

Patting Roan on the back, Billie said, "Good job, but I need to ask you another favour."

"What is it?" Roan asked as they strolled back to the bag together.

Billie opened the bag; inside were dozens of steel smallswords.

He picked up a sword and said, "I need you to train everyone how to fight and survive. Give these smallswords to whoever is most well trained."

He handed the bag to Roan, who replied, "Okay, is that all?"

Billie smiled and replied, "For now."

When everyone had finished working, Billie and Roan walked to the centre of the camp, where they had left the bag. The people in the camp saw them and walked over to them.

Billie announced loudly, "Everybody, Roan is going to teach you how to fight."

From the crowd, Sarabella asked, "Why do we need to learn how to fight?"

Billie responded, "I have seen what's out there just beyond our walls. Sorry to have to tell you that Oliver was killed whilst we were collecting the swords. If the mutated men come and attack us, we need to be able to defend ourselves. Get some rest; we'll start training in an hour."

An hour later, Roan stood in the centre of the village, holding a long steel sword. Everyone gathered in a circle round him.

He spoke loudly, "Get a partner and we will begin."

Some of the villagers didn't want to fight; they went to the lake outside the village, to collect water. Everyone else stood facing their partners. They all held smallswords. Billie partnered Roan. To the right of him was Lilly, holding her swords tightly with both hands. She was facing Sarabella, who held two small blades at her sides, waiting to begin. To the left of Billie was Leo, facing Isabelle.

When they were ready, Roan shouted, "People in my line will swing right, left, jab. Like this. The people opposite will try to block each attack with their swords, knocking them to the side. The attacker will walk forward, and the opponent will walk backward. We will start slowly before speeding it up; later, we'll switch. Watch me."

Roan showed them the moves, and then they began. Walking backward, Billie countered Roan's attacks. Sarabella countered Lilly, and Isabelle countered Leo's, then they switched.

From the centre, Roan shouted, "Faster now, and mix it up; throw your opponent off guard, knock them off balance, but don't cut anyone."

Roan kept attacking Billie with the same technique: right, left, jab. Billie knocked away the jab, but Roan kicked him to the ground and held his sword to Billie's throat. Billie conceded.

"You have to be ready for anything," Roan said.

Billie nodded, and Roan helped him up. Roan turned and saw Lilly attack Sarabella, right, left, then a jab. Sarabella kept blocking with her two swords.

Lilly tried to sweep her leg, but Sarabella saw it coming and stepped over and said, "My turn."

She came at Lilly aggressively, attacking quickly with her two swords. Lilly kept up with her pace, blocking her attacks. In the end, Sarabella knocked Lilly's sword to the side. She spun into her, elbowed her in the chest, and swept her left leg, knocking her to the ground.

Sarabella stopped, dropped her swords, knelt next to Lilly, and said, "OMG, I'm so sorry."

Lilly sat up and replied, "That's okay."

Roan jogged over to them, put his hand on Sarabella's shoulder, and said, "Just like Jenavieve."

Sarabella looked at Roan and asked, "You know my daughter?"

"Yes, I was her instructor. Your daughter attended my training camp."

Sarabella said, "Oh, you were her instructor; how did you make it back here?"

He helped Lilly to her feet, saying, "I got on a ship and came back."

He continued, "Remember what I said: be ready for anything."

Roan heard a clash of swords; he looked over and saw Leo attacking Isabelle. Isabelle fell backward and stumbled after every hit from her husband, who was very strong. Leo didn't want to hurt his wife, so he stopped and said, "Okay, your turn."

Isabelle swung at him, right, then left, and then a jab. She was weaker, and Leo could block her attacks with one hand. Isabelle saw that he was overconfident and took advantage of the situation. She swung right and then left as before, which he blocked, but then, she jumped up and kicked him in the stomach, knocking him to the ground.

Laughing, she helped him up and said, "Don't be overconfident; you won't always be fighting me."

He hugged her and agreed, "True."

Roan clapped his hands to get everyone's attention. "Good job today; we'll continue training tomorrow. Put the weapons back, and thanks."

The scout that Billie had sent out earlier to survey the land and see what was out there had returned.

The scout told Billie, "We're in trouble. I saw lots of mutated men close by and also many people, maybe a village full, both heading towards us. The villagers were led by a woman, and they didn't look friendly."

"How far?" Billie asked.

"They're on foot, but I think they'll be here quite soon."

Billie looked at Roan and asked, "If they attack, we won't be ready in time, will we?"

Roan replied, "No, we won't. And we don't stand a chance if the mutated men come. If they both attack, we'll need the people I trained at the training camp. Maybe, somehow, we will get lucky."

Chapter 14

The Creature

Angalie, Jenavieve, and Josh started their trek north in search of their parents.

They were with their new friend Theo, who said, "After we make it to the top of that mountain, it should be an easy journey."

From behind, Josh asked, "Is it a hard climb to the top of the mountain?"

Theo looked back at him with a weary face and replied, "I'm not sure."

They trudged on up the mountain, dragging their feet. The terrain was rough. As they got higher, they could see for miles ahead. The air was cold and damp.

They stopped when they neared the top and looked out at the scenery. Angalie said, "Wow, what a view."

No one replied, they just looked out at the sunlit landscape in awe.

They climbed higher and higher until they were shrouded in clouds. The clouds were thick, which reduced their visibility. Snow had fallen, and ice had formed on the ground, which made it slippery. They often lost their footing.

Theo was leading the way when all of a sudden, he slipped and tumbled down the mountainside, shouting back to the others as he fell. He hit his head on a rock, knocking him unconscious. The other three quickly knelt down, so as not to slip off the path, and peered down the mountain.

Angalie spotted him first. "There, I see him by those rocks. Looks like he's been knocked out," she called out, pointing.

Jenavieve scanned the area for a way down to him. "Back there," she said, indicating the way they had come. "There's a path which leads to him."

They hurried to the path and cautiously made their way down to Theo. When they got to him, Jenavieve crouched down by his head and shook him gently to wake him.

Josh asked, "You okay?"

Theo replied, "Yeah, I just banged my head, but not too hard."

Theo picked up the rock he hit his head on and noticed markings on it. They all looked at the rock, and Theo said, "I've seen these markings before."

"What do they mean?" Josh asked.

Theo looked at him and replied, "I haven't got a clue."

Jenavieve asked, "Can we carry on along this path?"

Theo stood up, looked down the path, and said, "Yeah, I think so. This way will lead us to where we want to go. The clouds are breaking up now, which is good."

They continued along the path and neared the bottom of the mountain.

Angalie saw something in the distance. "What's that?" she asked, pointing at it.

Jenavieve replied, "It looks like a castle. I wonder if anyone is inside."

Theo said, "I doubt it; it looks derelict."

"Let's go and see," suggested Angalie.

They set off at a fast pace and soon were standing in front of the castle doors. Theo pulled the doors open and walked inside into the main hall. The castle was cold and dark and appeared to be abandoned.

Josh shouted loudly, "Anybody here?"

The sound echoed through the castle, but there was no reply.

Theo looked around the main hall and said, "Let's split up and explore."

Nodding in agreement, Josh left with Angalie, while Theo and Jenavieve walked down some stone steps together.

As they approached a heavy door, Theo asked, "Shall we take a look inside?"

Jenavieve pushed the door, and it slowly creaked open.

"Looks like a dungeon," she said.

She stepped inside; Theo followed her. Looking around, they could see bones and chains scattered on the ground; it was full of cobwebs.

"I guess no one's here," she said.

Theo picked up a bone and saw that there were teeth marks on it.

"It looks like these people were eaten by some sort of animal."

Jenavieve took the bone from Theo; looking at the marks, she replied, "These are pretty big teeth marks. I hope that animal isn't still here. Let's go."

They stepped out and climbed the stairs back up to the main hall.

While Jenavieve and Theo were in the dungeon, Josh and Angalie had made their way to the armoury on the second floor. Angalie advanced to the wooden door of the armoury and yanked it open. There were swords and shields and spears stacked up against the walls.

As they looked around, they heard a noise behind them. In an instant, they turned but the sound stopped. They crept up to the door and looked outside to see what it was, but they could see nothing.

"Time to get back," Josh said.

Walking down the stairs back to the main hall, they met up with Theo and Jenavieve.

"Did you guys hear that sound?" Angalie asked them.

"What sort of sound?" Jenavieve replied.

Looking back the way they had come, Josh said, "There was a noise that came from up there; it sounded like *swish*."

"Maybe it was the wind," Theo said, following Josh's gaze up the steps.

They heard the sound again, louder this time, and Josh said, "You must have heard it then!"

Theo nervously replied, "Yeah, I definitely heard it then. I think we all did."

The four of them huddled together.

Theo asked, "What do you think it was?"

Josh turned to Theo and said, "I don't know, and I don't really want to find out."

"I agree," Angalie said as she locked arms with him.

Jenavieve separated herself from the huddle and said, "We have to find a way out of here."

Theo said, "If we can get out of here, then the rest of the journey through the mountains should be pretty straightforward."

At that moment, a howl emanated from the second floor. They turned and looked at each other, petrified.

Angalie said, "That sounded like a wolf."

"Yeah," Josh replied.

"Let's try to find a way out of here," Theo said.

They rushed out of the main hall and came to another room with a dining table in the centre. Theo went over to it, followed by the others. On the table were bowls filled with human bones. The room stank of rotting flesh.

Masking his nose and mouth with his hands, Theo muttered, "These bones have the same teeth marks as the bones in the dungeons."

Jenavieve picked up one of the bones to examine it and agreed, "Yeah, you're right."

Another loud howl came from behind them.

They turned around, and Josh said, "We need to get out of here. Whatever made that noise is getting closer."

Pointing past the table to the far corner of the room, Angalie called out, "Look, there's a door."

The four of them rushed to the door in the corner.

Jenavieve grabbed the handle and tried to open it.

"It's jammed."

Another even louder howl echoed around the room, stopping them in their tracks. A black and brown wolf-like creature was standing on two legs. It had huge claws, and its fangs were menacing. It had pointed ears and its hair was wavy like a dog's. The creature had a muscular humanoid body. As it leered at them, panting heavily with its mouth open and its tongue dripping saliva, they could see its breath in the cold air of the castle. Jenavieve had turned around and was desperately pulling on the door, trying to open it.

Not taking his eyes off the creature, Theo frantically, whispered, "How's that door coming along?"

Jenavieve didn't reply. The creature started to stalk them, taking slow, deliberate steps, still breathing heavily. When it reached the table, the creature let out an ear-splitting roar, spreading out its arms and baring its sharp teeth and claws.

Jenavieve yanked at the door again and again and with a loud thud she finally got it open. The creature charged at the four of them. Jenavieve ran through the open door into the fresh air. The others followed her out, slamming the door closed behind them.

Outside, Jenavieve spotted a rope bridge leading across a ravine.

She ran to the bridge and called out to the others, "C'mon, let's go this way."

Angalie and Josh followed her, got to the bridge, and started to cross. Theo was last onto the bridge. He was running backward in order to keep an eye on the castle for any sign of the creature. There was another loud roar, and the creature smashed through the door. It roared yet again and ran towards them.

"Run," Theo yelled as the creature leapt onto the bridge and started to rock it from side to side whilst striding towards them.

Jenavieve, Josh, and Angalie got to the other side of the bridge and waited for Theo. The creature was still rocking the bridge as Theo clambered towards his friends. Theo had almost reached the end of the bridge when the ropes gave way, and the bridge began to flip-flop down the mountainside. The creature was too heavy for the ancient rope bridge and it lost its footing. Theo was about to fall, but Josh grabbed his hand, just in the nick of time. The creature stretched its arm out as it fell and tried to grab Theo's leg, but Josh pulled him free, and the creature disappeared into the ravine.

Josh kept a firm grip on Theo's hand and called out to Jenavieve, "Help me pull him up."

She reached down and grabbed Theo's other hand, and they pulled him up to safety. Theo's heart was racing as he lay on the ground.

He exhaled and then said quietly, "Thank you."

Josh and Jenavieve helped him to his feet.

Jenavieve asked, "What was that thing?"

Angalie answered. "It looked like a wolf-man!"

Josh said, "Yeah, like a werewolf."

When Theo had got his breath back, Josh asked, "Do you know the way from here?"

"Yeah, I think so," he said. "It shouldn't be far now."

Once they'd all calmed down they continued on. The air was cool on the mountain but it wasn't too cold. The snow was beginning to melt. Looking into the distance, they could see more mountains. Josh saw some movement ahead.

He turned to Jenavieve and asked, "What's that?"

"It looks like people. They seem to be heading north too."

"We don't have to go that way, do we?" Angalie asked, not taking her eyes off the people.

"I'm afraid so, that's the only way."

Jenavieve said, "We might be able to find a way around them when we get to the bottom of this mountain."

They resumed their journey; after a while, as they neared the bottom, they saw four people sitting on the ground.

Angalie wondered, "Who are they?"

Josh replied, "Not sure, they don't look like the people we saw earlier."

They continued walking towards the four. As they came nearer, Jenavieve recognise who they were and started sprinting towards them.

"I know them," she yelled. "Follow me."

Chapter 15

Preparing to Fight

"Ashlie," Jenavieve shouted excitedly, as she ran over to her sister and knocked her to the ground, giving her a big hug.

Jenavieve hugged her sister tighter and started to tear up.

"Jenavieve," Ashlie cried; her eyes also streaming with tears of joy.

They sat on the hard gravel, ignoring the pain. They had their arms wrapped around each other so tightly, they could barely breathe.

Angalie came over and sat next to Rosalie; she put her arm on her shoulder, smiled, and said, "Nice to see you're still alive."

Rosalie replied, "You too."

Josh and Jimmy were talking to Bellomie.

Josh asked, "How are you guys? It's been a while."

Bellomie replied, "A lot has happened, but we're okay."

Theo watched from a distance. He realised they all knew each other and didn't want to interrupt their greetings.

Damon watched from afar too. He turned and looked back at the way Silver had gone. The path she had taken was steep; it was so rocky and would have been hard for her to clamber up.

After a few moments, Damon ambled over to Jenavieve and jokingly said, "I kept your sister safe enough."

Jenavieve grabbed him by the shoulders and said seriously, "Thank you."

Eventually, Theo joined them and introduced himself, "Hi, I'm Theo." He continued, "Jenavieve told me where you want to go. I can help you. I know these routes well. We are going to have to be careful, though. We don't know what we might come across. Are you ready to get going?"

They stared at him for a moment and then agreed.

As they climbed the path, Jimmy said, "Silver was with us earlier, but she saw someone up the mountain and chased after him. We have to find her; she couldn't have gone too far."

"Silver was with you? That's good. I was afraid she was taken," Jenavieve said anxiously, "or worse."

As they went in search of Silver, they started on the rocky path up the mountain that she had taken. The slope was steep. The air was cool, and the sun shone brightly. The mountain levelled off as they neared the top. There were more rocks to climb around, until they came across a grassy area. Led by Theo, they walked slowly through the tall grass. Theo continued on a little farther and then stopped.

Raising his hand in a fist, he said, "There are two sets of footprints here; I think she's close by."

Theo knelt down and brushed away some of the dirt to make sure it was two sets. The others joined him.

Scrutinising the footprints, Jenavieve concurred. "You're right."

Theo stood up and started hurrying downhill at a faster pace whilst the others followed, trying to keep up with him. Looking down the mountain into the open, they could see a forest which they assumed was where Silver had gone. The path ahead was rough; there were stones littering the ground. It was hard for them not to lose their balance. They trod carefully, trying not to stumble. As they neared the forest, the grass was not so tall and there were lots of trees and shrubs. They could hear birds singing. Theo examined the earth but there were hundreds of footsteps, so it was impossible to tell where Silver had gone. With all the trees in the forest, they couldn't see too far ahead.

Theo, unsure of what to do, said, "I guess we keep going and hope we find her."

Jimmy replied for everyone, "Yeah, let's keep going."

They continued walking through the trees and the thick forest. They marched on until they came to a clearing. Theo stopped to see if there was any sign of the direction Silver might have taken. Examining the ground, he noticed that there was a single set of footprints leading away from the other prints.

He called to Jenavieve.

"Could this be her?" Theo asked, indicating the footprints.

Jenavieve knelt down and looked at the prints; she brushed the loose soil away with her hands and replied, "It could be."

Drawing lines in the soft earth, she showed Theo the direction in which the two parties had gone.

"It looks like she went that way," Jenavieve said, pointing as she stood up.

The footprints Silver had left led up the slope. As they followed the tracks, Theo watched carefully to make sure he didn't lose them. Beyond a thicket of trees, though, he lost the trail and paused. Jenavieve caught up and stopped next to him.

"What's wrong?" she asked.

Jimmy arrived too; he took a deep breath, looked down, and said, "The footprints have vanished."

The three of them huddled together; Jenavieve asked, "Where do you think she went?"

Theo replied, "I think she's still heading north, but avoiding people."

They were all tired from the long trek.

Angalie rested her arm on Jimmy's shoulder and asked, "What should we do?"

Theo replied, "I think that we should carry on along this path. It will lead us north, and hopefully, we'll find her along the way."

So, they continued along the path. Theo and Jenavieve led the way. They slowed when they saw a bed of roses which had been trodden down. Theo noticed that Silver's footprints had resurfaced.

It had started to drizzle, which made the path muddy. As they walked through the mud, Theo and Jenavieve heard someone ahead of them. They sped up to a jog.

They came to another clearing and Jenavieve spotted Silver and a man she didn't recognise and a mutant, facing off. Jenavieve figured the man must have been from the village. Theo and Jenavieve stood motionless with the rest of the group as Silver leapt forward and swung her sword at the villager's chest. He blocked it and pushed her back. Without warning, the mutant sprang at Silver. She caught the creature by the neck and threw it to the ground, slashing its arm as it fell. The mutant turned in a frenzy and dived at the villager, knocking him to the ground and gouging his face and biting at his throat. The mutant tossed the lifeless body aside. With its face and teeth covered in blood, the creature turned towards Silver, letting out an ear-piercing screech.

Jimmy sprinted towards the two of them, hurling his sword at the mutant. The sword span through the air and skewered the creature through the chest. The mutant swayed for a moment and then fell to its knees and slumped to the ground.

Jimmy exclaimed, "Wow. Are you okay, Silver?"

Looking at the two lifeless bodies on the ground, she smiled and said, "Yeah, thanks. I see you picked up some stragglers."

Jimmy pulled his sword out of the mutant and cleaned it on his shorts. He replied, "Yep, that's Theo; he's been keeping Angalie, Josh, and Jenavieve safe."

The others joined Jimmy and Silver. They were sickened by the sight of the mangled, dead bodies.

Pointing at the dead man Bellomie broke the silence, "He must have been a scout or something from the village, sent to come and find us."

Theo added, "We need to carry on. I don't think it's far now."

Including Silver, they were now ten. They trudged along the muddy path in the drizzling rain, through another clearing, and carried on until they came to more trees, which gave them shelter. In the distance, they could see Coralie's camp, with the villagers resting in tents. It was growing dark.

Bellomie said, "Let's go this way and stay hidden in the trees; we don't want them to see us."

Moving stealthily through the trees, they made sure they weren't seen. They walked beyond the trees and kept out of sight. Eventually, they saw a gate and a wall in the distance.

Jenavieve said, "Looks like that could be where our parents are. They must have rebuilt it."

Josh said, "Yeah, that's a large gate, and it looks like there's a moat around the wall."

Holding their hands over their heads to keep dry, they strode on through the mud and eventually got to the moat. Looking up, they saw that there were torches lit around the wall. Billie stood at the top of the wall, looking down at them.

He called out, "Who goes there?"

Jimmy looked up at Billie and shouted, "Billie, it's Jimmy."

Billie stared for a few seconds before he recognised Jimmy in the dark and then commanded, "Lower the drawbridge."

The drawbridge was lowered, and they trudged in. Billie jumped off the wall and greeted them.

Exhausted, all Jimmy could say was, "Billie."

Billie smiled and said, "Jimmy."

Angalie asked, "Have you seen any people from the surrounding villages?"

"Not many, but Roan and your parents are here. I'm sure you want to see them."

Ashlie grabbed her sister's hand tightly and asked, "Mum is here?"

"Yup, follow me, I'll take you to them and get you some tents."

They went straight to Sarabella's tent. She was lying on the floor, fast asleep.

Billie walked in and said, "I'll let you guys be."

Jenavieve dashed over to her mother and shook her. Ashlie knelt beside her. Sarabella woke, looked up at them and couldn't believe her eyes. She thought that she must be dreaming. She gabbed both of them and pulled them to her and hugged them tightly.

"I missed you both so much."

Ashlie replied, "We missed you too, Mum"

Kissing both of them on their heads, their mother asked, "How are you both?"

Jenavieve began crying with joy at seeing her mother again.

"A lot has happened, but it's better now."

"Come lie down, we'll get some rest and you can tell me all about it," Sarabella said as she lay down on the ground, holding her daughters.

Billie took Josh to the next tent to see his mother, who was awake and twirling her sword, with the point of the blade against the ground.

Billie said to Josh, "She's inside."

"Thanks."

Josh walked in and saw his mum. Lilly turned when she heard the tent flap open; she dropped her sword, ran to her son, and hugged him firmly. "My sweet, sweet boy," she said. "How are you? I've been so worried."

With his arms still wrapped around her, Josh replied, "I'm good, Mum. We're safe now."

They lay down on top of some clothes and tried to get to sleep. Lilly was wrapped in Josh's arms.

Next, Billie took Angalie to her parents' tent. Leo and Isabelle were sleeping.

Angalie walked in and called out, "Mum, Dad."

They woke instantly. Isabelle sat up and cried out, "Angalie!"

She ran and hugged them both.

"How have you been?" Isabelle asked.

Filled with joy, Angalie replied, "I've been all right; my friends and I protected each other."

"We're so glad you're safe," Leo said.

The three of them lay down and got some rest.

Billie led the remaining six people to an empty tent.

"Follow me," he said. "You can share this tent. There are six beds, one for each of you."

The beds were just soft sheets on the floor spread around the tent.

"Thanks," Bellomie replied as he took a seat on one of the sheets.

He was joined by his sister Rosalie. They tried to rest but couldn't stop thinking about the mutants and Coralie and her villagers.

In the morning, the sun shone brightly again. Billie was the first to wake. He strolled out of his tent, shading his eyes with his hand. Roan came out of his tent and joined him. The others joined them shortly after.

Billie had sent a scout out the night before to look for anything dangerous. The scout returned and reported to Billie.

"There is a group of people and some mutants not too far from here."

This news worried Billie.

"How long do you think it will take them to get here?"

The scout was worried too; he said, "I don't know. It could be very soon, depending on when they leave. The mutants were a lot closer, but they weren't heading in this direction."

Billie turned to Roan, who stared back at him and nodded his head as he thought.

"We should prepare for the worst," Roan said, looking towards the people who had been training and who were listening to their conversation.

Jimmy asked Roan and Billie, "Have you been training everyone the same way you trained us?"

Roan said, "Yes, we have all been training, including your parents. If the mutants come, we all need to be ready."

He pointed to each person he had been training and partnered them up. "Get your weapons, and let's show your children what we've learned."

Sarabella, Lilly, Leo, and Isabelle walked past their children and picked up weapons; the others who had been training joined them. Billie faced Roan. Lilly faced Sarabella, and Leo faced Isabelle. Roan gave the order to begin.

The youngsters watched as their parents started swinging their swords at each other, walking forward, then switching and walking backward. They trained for half an hour. Then it was the children's turn to join in. They paired up and practised their moves, swinging from left, then right, then stab. They continued this for another half-hour.

After they finished, everyone gathered around Roan, who spoke loudly, "This is just training; if the mutants attack, it will be very different. They won't hold back; they will go for the kill. It's kill or be killed. So, you have to be alert and ready when the time comes. We must protect each other, no matter the cost. If you see someone hurt or losing their fight, help them."

Roan spoke with determination in his voice. Everyone listened intently. After he finished speaking, they put away their weapons. It was midday, time for lunch and thinking about what Roan had said.

Whilst eating lunch Jimmy heard noises in the distance. He turned away from the others, looked at the gate, and tried to focus on the sounds.

He turned back and said, "I can hear something; I think they're close."

He stood up and went to the main gate. The others followed him. He climbed to the top of the wall and looked out. In the far distance, to the right, he could see the mutants, and closer to him, he recognised the people from Coralie's village.

Jimmy looked down and told the others, "They're here."

Earlier, Billie had told everyone where to stand if the mutated men arrived.

He climbed to the top of the wall beside the gate, stood next to Jimmy, and called out, "Get your weapons, take your positions, and be ready. They're coming. Remember your training, and protect each other."

Billie turned and looked out at the approaching mutants. He was nervous; his hands started shaking as he saw them slowly getting closer. Jimmy grabbed Billie's hands and said, "It's going to be okay; we've had a lot of training."

Billie nodded and replied, "Okay," knowing it wasn't going to be okay.

He turned to Josh and told him to man the wall. Josh slowly climbed the ladder and stood next to Jimmy. Billie climbed down. As the mutants came into the open, Jimmy could see there were so many of them. The sword slipped out of Jimmy's hand.

Looking out at the mutated men, Josh croaked, "That's a lot of mutants!"

In the distance, Coralie and her villagers were watching the mutants fearfully.

Chapter 16

Fight or Flight

Dark rain clouds had unexpectedly formed, dimming the light over the rebuilt village. The air grew cool, it started to rain and the ground became muddy. The people inside the wall waited nervously to see what would happen between the mutants and Coralie's villagers. Josh and Jimmy stood on the wall above the gate. The rain was getting harder and harder. The water level in the moat was slowly rising.

Josh and Jimmy looked out and saw that the mutants were closing in on Coralie's villagers, who were still marching towards the moat. The mutants trudged slowly through the mud, drenched by the downpour. Coralie stopped at the moat and turned to face them. Josh and Jimmy stared down from the top of the wall, an uneasy feeling in their stomachs. They both felt nauseated and their hands started shaking.

Jimmy asked, "What do you think is going to happen?"

Josh stared at him blankly, uneasy about how to answer, and replied, "I don't know."

Jenavieve, her sister, and her mum were on the ground below Jimmy and Josh. The three of them had found a tiny hole in the wall to look through. Sarabella's sword was tucked into her belt, and she had her arms around her daughters. She could tell they were just as frightened as she was.

Sarabella spoke calmly, hoping to reassure both girls, "Whatever happens, you protect each other."

Ashlie replied, "Okay."

The three of them watched as the mutants squelched through the mud towards the moat. Angalie was with her Mum and Dad. They were holding each other, feeling afraid. Billie, Theo and Damon joined Josh and Jimmy on the wall above the gate. The five of them stood and waited. Bellomie, Rosalie, and Silver were inside the gate with their swords drawn; they waited anxiously with the others. Angalie and her parents had joined them behind the gate. They all shook with fear as they listened to the mutants' screeches.

The mutants were menacingly advancing on Coralie's villagers. Billie looked down at Roan and said,

"Roan, take charge there on the ground. I'll tell you what's happening outside the wall."

The five on the wall kept a firm gaze out at the two groups in front of them. The mutants pounded the ground, let out loud screeches, and charged the villagers.

Jimmy asked, "Shouldn't we help them?"

They all stared for a moment, speechless, not knowing what they should do.

As more screeches filled their ears, Roan yelled, "What's going on out there?"

Still in shock, Billie shouted, "The mutated men are charging towards the villagers."

Sarabella shouted above the noise of the screeching, "Open the gates and let them in."

"No, we can't," Damon cried out. "If we let them in they'll kill us all."

Sarabella replied, "We can't just let them die out there."

"What should we do?" Lilly asked, looking up to the men on the wall.

Billie thought for a moment and then climbed down the ladder.

He shouted up to Damon and the others, "I'll open the gate and lower the drawbridge; if we don't help them, the mutants will slaughter the villagers."

Billie and Roan started to wind down the drawbridge. As it opened, Jimmy could see that the mutants were almost upon the villagers. Jimmy jumped down from the wall and sprinted out to help Coralie and her villagers. Coralie was leading from the front as always and closest to the mutants, with her sword out in front of her, ready to defend herself and her people. Her villagers were behind her, some with weapons, and some without. They were all terrified as screeches reverberated through the air.

Coralie's advisors stood next to her with their swords drawn. One of the mutants charged at her. Before it could reach her, an advisor jumped forward and hacked it down. Instantly, more ran forward and jumped on the advisor, ripping him to shreds. His blood spurted all over Coralie and the other advisor. They watched the mutants bite at his body and tear it apart like a pack of rabid dogs. The advisor and Coralie stepped back. The mutant's heads, mouths, and claws were covered in blood. They licked their lips and stared at Coralie and the villagers.

"*Run!*" Coralie heard from behind. She turned to see who had shouted and then ran back towards them. Her advisor was slow to react, and a mutant grabbed his leg and bit into his calf. The advisor yelled in pain.

He shouted for help but was instantly covered in mutants.

After taking one last glance back at her advisor, Coralie rushed to re-join her villagers.

Jimmy ran over to Coralie and shouted, "There are too many to fight."

Coralie replied, "We can't outrun them; we need to get inside."

The villagers heard Coralie but they ignored her and started running in the opposite direction, heading for the mountains.

"Roan, what should we do?" Billie asked, nervous and breathing heavily.

Roan stared silently at the mutants.

"I'm out of here," Coralie cried. Fearing for her life; she ran after her villagers.

Finding himself alone outside the wall except for the mutants, Jimmy sprinted back to the drawbridge to re-join his friends.

"If we stay here and the mutants get in we'll be trapped. I guess we should follow her," Roan finally said. "They'll need protecting. Let's go."

The rain picked up. Leaving their newly rebuilt village, Roan, Billie, Jimmy and the rest started running towards the mountains too. Only the Screechers followed them, squelching through the mud on all fours like dogs. The mutated men took shelter in the trees. Jimmy chased after Coralie. Isabella, Leo, and Angalie lagged behind. Angalie turned to see if the Screechers were still following. She shrieked when she saw they were right behind them, "Mum, run! They're right behind us."

The Screechers crawled on all fours but moved fast. One of them grabbed Isabella's foot. She took out her sword and hacked at it. It let go, grabbed her thigh, and took a bite out of her calf. She fell to the ground, but Leo knocked the mutant off her and helped her up. Angalie put her mother's arm over her back, and they limped on, trying to catch up with the others. Angalie called for help but no one heard her.

Straightaway, three more Screechers jumped on their backs, knocking them to the ground. Angalie grabbed her sword and stabbed one creature in the chest, killing it. She turned and looked at her parents, who were in trouble. The other two Screechers were on top of them, clawing at them. Angalie saw more Screechers approaching in the distance. She got up, kicked the creature off her mother, and then ran up to her father and punched his attacker in the face.

"We've got to go," Angalie cried. "More are coming."

Her parents were bleeding from their hands and legs and faces. Angalie called to the others to help her again. Theo and Rosalie were first to get to them.

"Help me get her up," Theo said to Rosalie.

The two of them picked up Isabella whilst Angalie helped her father.

The Screechers were right behind them again. Rosalie and Theo were dragging Isabella, but her foot was bleeding badly. She was in too much pain to keep going.

With the Screechers almost upon them, she said, "Stop. Put me down. I can't go on."

Rosalie and Theo laid her down, drew their swords, and faced the approaching Screechers, ready to defend her.

Angalie and Leo were just in front; they stopped and came back.

"You have to keep going," Angalie said, holding her mother's shoulder.

Isabella grabbed her hand and said, "I can't; you guys go on. I will only slow you down."

"We're not going to just leave you here," Leo said.

Isabella let go of Angalie, pulled Leo down on one knee, and whispered in his ear, "We're not gonna survive; the best we can do is protect Angalie."

As she finished talking, she realised it was already too late.

Chapter 17

Are They Safe?

The Screechers were upon them. Angalie drew her sword and ran to Theo to help him fight.

"Angalie. No!" Leo shouted from the ground.

He was holding Isabella, who had passed out from the pain. He held her head in his hand and checked her pulse. She had stopped breathing. He tried to resuscitate her, but nothing happened; she was gone.

"On your right," Angalie shouted at Rosalie.

Rosalie turned and saw two Screechers leap towards her. She caught one of them with her sword and impaled it. As she pulled the sword out, the other Screecher clawed at her stomach, leaving three bloody lines across it. She stumbled backward, holding her stomach.

The creature let out a screech and charged at Rosalie again. It jumped towards her trying to slash her throat. To protect her, Theo sprang between Rosalie and the Screecher, knocking her to the ground, but before he could react to the creature it slit his throat with its claws. As blood spurted out, Theo clutched his throat and tried in vain to stop the bleeding. He fell to his knees, gasping for air.

The Screecher turned back to Rosalie. She was still holding her stomach and staring blankly at Theo's body. She started to crawl away, but the mutant pounced on her. Rosalie held up her hands to defend her face. It started clawing at her hands; her eyes were closed.

The clawing stopped! She opened her eyes and saw Bellomie stabbing the Screecher repeatedly.

He walked over to his sister. Rosalie's hands were covered in blood and her stomach had three huge claw marks across it.

Rosalie looked at her stomach and bloody hands and said, "Bellomie, I'm not gonna make it; you have to go, leave me."

Bellomie hugged her tightly and said, "I can't leave you."

"You have to," she replied, squeezing her brother's hand and then letting it go.

Bellomie looked at the approaching Screechers and then back at his sister. He bowed his head and said a prayer, knowing he couldn't fight them all.

Angalie finished killing her two attackers and ran to join Bellomie and Rosalie.

She said, "Guys, we need to get out of here."

"She's not going anywhere," Bellomie said, pointing at his sister.

Angalie looked at Rosalie's wounds and realised she couldn't walk.

Rosalie said, "Leave me here; you two need to go. There's no point all of us dying."

Angalie and Bellomie stared at her in shock. They were distraught by what she had said, but more Screechers were coming, and they had to act quickly.

"Bellomie, let's go," Angalie said, grabbing his shoulder.

He brushed her hand off and gave his sister a big hug.

A tear trickled down his cheek as he said, "I will always love you."

Rosalie patted him on the back and whispered, "You too, big brother, now go."

Angalie and Bellomie raced away. Hearing the loud screeches, they figured that the creatures had reached Rosalie, but they didn't dare look. They heard her scream as the Screechers clawed and bit her. They tried to block out the noise by holding their hands over their ears as they ran to catch up with Leo, Angalie's father. They saw that his cuts were serious, and he was barely moving.

"Dad!" Angalie cried as they approached him.

Leo lay on the ground. Angalie sprinted to his side.

"Try to keep your eyes open," Angalie said as she gently stroked his head.

"Angalie, I don't feel so …" Leo's eyes closed again. He'd lost consciousness.

Angalie shook him, but there was no response. She looked at Bellomie, devastated.

"Is he alive?" he asked.

She shook him again, but there was still no response.

"Is he breathing?"

Angalie checked his wrist for a pulse, but there was none.

She lied, saying, "Barely."

The Screechers were getting closer.

Frantic, Bellomie said, "We need to decide what to do."

Angalie squeezed her father's hand, apologised in her heart, and said, "Let's go."

Bellomie and Angalie hurried on, towards the mountain. Jimmy and the others were just ahead, and they rushed to join them. Jimmy was at the back; he turned when he heard Angalie approach. He could see tears in her eyes.

Jimmy ran to Angalie, hugged her and asked, "What's wrong? What happened? Where are your parents?"

Angalie wiped her nose, dried the tears from her eyes, and said, "They're dead, killed by the Screechers."

Jimmy hugged her again and turned to Bellomie and asked, "Rosalie and Theo?"

Bellomie shook his head, crying silently.

"Sorry," Jimmy said.

They continued walking up the mountain and reached the others, who were waiting for them.

With tears in her eyes and in a croaky voice, Angalie asked, "What's going on?"

Billie was the first to reply, "Coralie is just ahead, but she's stopped."

They stood together watching Coralie and then cautiously advanced towards her. Coralie took a quick glance behind at them and then continued staring out in front of her.

Damon stepped forward and asked, "Coralie, what are you …"

He stopped in mid-sentence, as he could see what she was looking at. In the distance was the sea and an offshore island. The others had caught up with Damon and Coralie by now. Coralie's villagers were sprinting down the mountain towards the sea.

"It looks like people may be living there," Silver said.

Jenavieve walked up to Damon and commented, "Yeah. Seems like it wasn't destroyed by the meteors. We'll need to decide what to do now."

A few silent moments passed. Coralie was gripping her short sword tightly.

Damon broke the silence and taking a few slow steps towards her, said "Put your sword down, Coralie, we're not going to hurt you."

Their eyes were locked on each other. Coralie kept a firm grip on the sword but then decided it wasn't worth dying over. She looked down the mountain at her villagers, who had abandoned her.

She dropped to her knees, thinking about her sister and murmured, "Sorry, I couldn't save you."

Tears fell down her cheeks.

Bellomie and Angalie looked behind; the Screechers had stopped following.

"There's no way back," Angalie said. "We need to continue towards the sea."

Billie replied, "Yeah, I think you're right."

Coralie had already started walking down the mountainside.

"We should follow her," Damon suggested to the others.

"Yeah, I guess so," Roan agreed.

As they neared the sea, Coralie's villagers were still in sight; they had gathered beside a ship that they'd discovered anchored nearby.

"We can use that to get to the island," Billie shouted, increasing his pace.

Coralie was still ahead of them; she was also heading straight for the ship where her villagers had stopped.

In her mother tongue, Coralie said, *"We are going to take this ship to the island."*

Jimmy and the others reached the beach; they were all out of breath.

"How are we gonna get on?" Ashlie asked.

Jenavieve answered her sister, "Not sure; maybe there's a gangplank or something."

"I doubt anyone is on board," Jimmy said. "It looks abandoned."

Coralie took command, "We will check the port side of the ship; you guys check the starboard."

"C'mon, let's go," Billie said, as he waded into the sea, followed by the others.

"Ow!" Josh cried, after stepping on a sharp stone.

"There's a lot of stones," Silver warned.

She jumped up onto a sandbank and found herself standing next to Roan.

He looked down at the clear blue sea and said, "Try to avoid them."

Silver nodded.

"I think I see a way to get on board," Jimmy said as he splashed through the breakers towards the ship.

The others followed. They waded through the water; the waves crashing against them. Jimmy had spotted a rope hanging down from the ship's handrail. He waited for the others, who were slowly catching up with him.

Jimmy pointed to the rope and said, "We can use that to climb up to get on board."

He grabbed the rope and began to shimmy up it. When he got to the top, he turned and called to them to come on board.

The others were taking a long time to climb the rope so Jimmy decided to explore the ship. By the time Billie had clambered on board, Jimmy was walking along one of the lower decks. It was dark but spacious; his footsteps echoed as he walked. He heard something in the distance ahead. He thought about turning back. He got his bearings then carried on into the dark. Jimmy came to a sunlit corridor and saw Coralie; he assumed that she had made the noise.

"Coralie," Jimmy said.

Coralie turned and asked, "What?"

Jimmy was startled by her abrupt reply but continued, "Have you found any way to start the ship?"

"No, obviously not," she replied.

"If we can make it up to the bridge, we can start it from there; what do you think?"

"Fine," Coralie agreed. "Follow me."

The two of them walked along the corridor and Coralie found a door which fortunately led up to the bridge. They walked in and looked around.

"I don't see any controls," Jimmy said.

"Here, maybe this lever will do it," Coralie called out.

Jimmy strolled over and looked at the lever.

"Try pulling it," he suggested.

She did so, but nothing happened. They were unsure of what to do next.

They stood thinking for a moment and then Coralie pulled the lever and flicked a switch that she had just discovered. There was a loud noise, and the engine exploded into life.

"You did it," Jimmy yelled.

"Take the wheel and head for the island." Coralie ordered, looking through the window of the bridge out to sea.

There was a sudden jerk. Jimmy let go of the wheel and fell to the ground; Coralie also fell.

Jimmy asked, "You okay?"

Coralie pushed herself up and said, "Yeah, what was that?"

Jimmy replied. "We hit a sandbank but it's okay now."

Coralie helped him up, and Jimmy regained control of the wheel.

"Where are your friends?" she asked.

Still holding the wheel and trying to keep the ship steady, he replied, "I don't know; last I saw, they were coming on board."

The others were already on board and decided to look around the ship themselves. They were walking on the lower deck when suddenly the ship hit something, and they all fell to the ground.

"What was that?" Jenavieve asked.

Josh had fallen next to her; he replied, "I don't know. Maybe we hit a wave or the engine stalled."

They got up and carried on all the way round the ship till they came into the open air again. They could now see the villagers who were looking off the stern of the ship. Angalie spotted a staircase to their right, which led to another deck.

Pointing to it, Angalie said, "Let's go and check this out."

Jenavieve and Josh followed her.

Billie said, "Okay, you three go and see what's down there; we'll talk to the villagers. Hopefully one of them can speak English."

They parted ways. Jenavieve, Josh, and Angalie got to the staircase; Angalie made her way down first, Josh and Jenavieve behind.

"It's pretty dark down here," Angalie said as she reached the bottom.

Arriving on the steerage deck, the lowest deck on the boat, Josh asked, "What is this place?"

"I don't know," Angalie replied. "It's too dark to tell."

Jenavieve pulled a lighter from her pocket and said, "This will help."

She clicked her lighter on and lifted it in the air, saying, "Follow me."

Angalie said, "This looks like a prison cell."

"Yeah," Josh replied, gripping the bars.

Jenavieve moved her lighter around to see if there was anything inside, but there wasn't. They continued looking into the rest of the cells and went around the whole deck but found nothing; so, they headed back upstairs to the others where Billie was in deep conversation with one of the villagers.

The three of them stopped just behind Billie and listened. He had just asked the villager what they thought would be waiting for them on the island. The villager, who spoke English, said he thought he saw people.

The ship began to slow as it approached the island. Everyone ran to the bow to get a better view.

They all gazed anxiously as the ship approached the sandy beach. They couldn't wait to find out what was ahead of them in this new land.

Chapter 18

The Island

Everyone disembarked and stepped onto the beach.

Jimmy looked into the distance and said, "It looks amazing. Let's explore."

He and Josh, Jenavieve, and Angalie headed off inland, towards the mountains, whilst the rest went to find any inhabitants of the island.

Meanwhile, Billie had spotted something.

"Look, up there," he shouted, pointing.

They all squinted into the distance but couldn't make out what it was.

Billie said, "I wonder if there are people up there."

"We will go and find out. Follow me," Coralie commanded.

They set off up the mountainside. Every step was nerve-racking. They were petrified that the mutants might be here. They hiked up into the woods in search of whatever Billie thought he had seen. Coming out of the woods into a clearing, they saw a large village. As they got closer, they could see that the village was rundown; they figured it must have been rebuilt hastily. Coralie was first to reach the entrance to the village. She approached a young girl and asked who was in charge. The girl pointed to one of the buildings near the back of the village. Coralie led the others there.

As they passed through the village, Coralie noticed that all the people were working hard. Some were in chains with guards barking orders at them.

"What's going on here?" Coralie wondered to herself.

The rest of them saw the chained villagers too and realised they had no idea what they just walked into. However, they continued till they reached the building.

A slim, old man greeted them at the door and said, "I don't recognise you. Where have you come from? How did you get here? Why are you here?"

Billie was about to speak but was interrupted by Coralie.

"We found a ship and used it to flee from the mutants on the mainland."

"Oh, you found my ship, I see. Thank you for bringing it back. My name is Bob. I'm the village elder."

Billie asked, "Do you have anywhere that we could sleep tonight?"

"We have a couple of empty houses where you and your people can stay, but some of you will have to share. Is that okay?"

Billie replied, "Yes, thanks."

Bob showed them their new homes and got them settled in. He gave them vouchers to get food. The last to get settled were Ashlie, Damon, and Sarabella.

Whilst unpacking, Ashlie said, "I hope Jenavieve gets back okay."

Sarabella replied, "I'm sure she'll be here soon. No need to worry."

Bob left them and closed the door behind him, turning a key to lock it with a click.

"What was that?" Ashlie asked.

Sarabella peered through the door's peephole and said, "I don't know. I can't see anything. Don't worry about it; I'm sure it's nothing. Let's get ready; we'll get something to eat soon."

"I hope Jimmy, Josh, Angalie, and Jenavieve are back in time for the food," Damon said.

"You two stop worrying," Sarabella said. "I'm sure they'll be back in no time. Now get ready."

Jimmy, Josh, Angalie, and Jenavieve had been walking for ages. They stopped when they saw a young boy. He had his back turned to them and was holding something in his hands.

"Is that a child?" Jenavieve asked, curiously.

Jimmy replied, "Yeah, looks like it."

"What's that he's holding?" Josh asked.

"It looks like a computer or something," Angalie responded.

Jimmy took a step towards the boy and said, "Wait, I think I've seen that before. I could have sworn that I saw Billie with a computer like that back at the village?"

"How did he get it?" Angalie asked.

Jimmy kept his gaze on the boy and replied, "No idea; let's ask."

But before they could do so, they saw movement in the trees.

"Run!" they shouted at the boy.

The boy turned and looked at them, unsure of why they had shouted. Moments later, three mutants were upon him. In the attack the computer was knocked from the boy's hands. It slid over the grass and stopped at Jimmy's feet. The mutants surrounded the boy and began clawing at him. Within seconds, he was dead, as they watched in horror. Jimmy snatched up the computer, and the four of them ran, chased by the mutants.

Breathing heavily, Josh asked Jimmy, "Do you know how to use that computer?"

Jimmy started pressing the keys as they ran, but nothing happened.

Josh suggested, "Maybe it's voice activated."

"Worth a shot. Find us a way out of here!"

The computer glowed, and a red dot lit up on the screen, showing a map of the island. Jimmy assumed it was showing him which way to go. The mutants were still chasing them. Following the dot on the computer, they ran down the mountain and continued on towards some trees.

"Follow me," Jimmy shouted.

The mutants were right behind them.

"We might be able to lose them in those trees," Jimmy called out.

They kept darting between the trees and got to a clearing. In front of them they could see a field that ended at the top of a cliff.

Angalie gasped, "There's a cliff ahead; we're trapped! Which way now?"

Jimmy stared at the computer and replied, "I'm not sure. I think we have to jump. That's what it's showing."

"That's ridiculous," Josh yelled. "There must be another way; ask it again."

The mutants came out of the trees. Jimmy slowed to a jog as he neared the edge of the cliff. He asked the computer again which way to go. This time, the red dot on the screen was even larger.

As they closed in on the cliff edge, Jimmy said, "We have to jump; that's what it's still showing me."

An Unfinished Event

They looked back at the approaching mutants and then at each other. The four of them linked arms, closed their eyes, and jumped.

The mutants didn't notice the edge of the cliff. The four friends hurtled through the air followed closely by the three mutants.

Jimmy prayed under his breath, "Please, God, save us."

The computer was emitting a vivid red light, illuminating their bodies. They felt weightless.

Next instant, they found themselves sitting on a patch of grass in a park.

Stunned by their fall, they stared in amazement at the people and the buildings.

"What happened?" Angalie asked. "How are we still alive?"

"Where's the cliff gone?" Jenavieve wondered.

Josh asked, "Where are we?"

Jimmy looked around, lost. "I don't understand."

Deus ex Machina

Lightning Source UK Ltd.
Milton Keynes UK
UKHW010216241120
373929UK00003B/991

9 781543 758511